Crying in the Dark

Ann Halam was born and raised in Manchester, and after graduating from Sussex University spent some years travelling throughout South East Asia. She now lives in Brighton with her husband and son. As well as being a children's author, Ann Halam writes adult science fiction and fantasy books, as Gwyneth Jones.

Other books by the same author from Orion

The Haunting of Jessica Raven
The Fear Man
The Powerhouse

Crying in the Dark

Ann Halam

A Dolphin Paperback

First published in Great Britain in 1998
as a Dolphin paperback
by Orion Children's Books
a division of the Orion Publishing Group Ltd
Orion House
5 Upper St Martin's Lane
London WC2H 9EA

A catalogue record for this book
is available from the British Library

Typeset at The Spartan Press Ltd,
Lymington, Hants

Printed in Great Britain
by Clays Ltd, St Ives plc.
ISBN 1 85881 394 8

Part One

One

ELINOR WAS HIDING FROM HER COUSINS. SHE HAD found an old hollow yew tree in the corner of the churchyard. Nathalie and Megan were playing on the gravestones by the church door, but their voices seemed to come from inside the tree: echoing like the sea-sounds you hear when you put a big shell to your ear. She heard Derek trying, as always, to get his sisters' attention: 'Look! Look at me! I can jump right over it.' Megan laughed loudly. Nathalie drawled, in a superior tone she'd copied from her mother. 'For heaven's sake, don't encourage him!' Then the sisters started talking more quietly, and she knew they were talking about her. 'Elinor –' she heard Nathalie say. 'Little creep. If she gets the idea that she can –' Megan answered: too low for Elinor to catch her words, but she could be sure Megan agreed with anything Nathalie proposed. Megan was nine: still a brash, fat little girl while her sister was a sleek and supposedly sophisticated teen-ager. She would be proud and eager to join in Nathalie's bullying plans.

The tree must be very old. Its ruined trunk was held together by bands of steel, and supported by steel braces fixed into the loamy, needly ground. The sounds of the past might be caught in that dark, damp cave. If only her cousins would shut up, words that had been spoken hundreds of years ago might whisper their secrets into Elinor's ear. But she didn't like confined spaces, and anyway a hollow tree wasn't a good place to hide. If you were caught you couldn't escape. She imagined Nathalie and Megan peering in through this rift in the trunk, bright-eyed and laughing: like two cats at a mousehole. That was definitely a prospect to be avoided.

In the yew's lightless shade there was one big tomb, standing alone on a rise in the ground beside an odd, shallow pool. Elinor managed to trace some of the lettering on the mossy slabs. It was the Revelle family vault apparently: and that was interesting because the holiday house, which they had yet to find, either belonged or had belonged to the Revelles, the traditional lords of the manor around here. Auntie Sylvia had rented it from an estate agent, but she'd been thrilled at the connection. She'd started talking about 'The Revelles' as if they were close friends, as if they'd practically invited her to come and stay. The tomb looked very neglected. If the Revelles were still the local gentry, there must be a newer one somewhere.

Her cousins' voices moved farther away. At the church door, Auntie Sylvia and Uncle Derek were having a conversation with someone: the verger or the vicar or maybe another tourist like themselves. Elinor sat with her back against the tomb, the pool on one side, the churchyard wall on the other; and beyond that a sweep of empty, sunny meadow. In the distance she could see the roofs, chimneys and windows of a big house peering out of a band of trees. But even if they'd been looking out of the windows it was too far away for anyone to see her. She felt safe. This was the kind of hiding place she liked: not too attractive, nothing here that anyone else would want; and not shut in. If she heard her cousins coming she'd have time to slip quietly behind the yew tree and get back to the relative security of her uncle and aunt's company before she was spotted. They weren't a reliable defence. If Elinor complained about the others, Auntie Sylvia would yell at her for 'telling tales'. But Nathalie and Megan never did anything too horrible while their parents were looking.

Out in the meadow it was a cloudless summer's day. Under the yew she seemed to be sitting in a darkened theatre looking up at a brightly-coloured stage set, as if she was waiting for a play to begin. But nothing was happening yet. *I can come here again*, she thought. *If it's near enough to walk*. They won't be able to say I'm hiding or sulking. I'm not hiding, I simply don't happen to be in plain sight. Any day when we don't all go out to the sea or somewhere, I can come to my secret yew tree and have some peace.

In many families somebody is bullied. Parents are unfair, one child is favoured and another teased and tormented. Maybe few children grow up without feeling – some time or other – that it's all a horrible mistake and they really belong to another, much nicer family. For Elinor part of that was the truth. She didn't belong: but there was no ideal family who might come and rescue her, and it was not romantic at all. She had lived with the Madisons since her father had been killed in a terrible fire when she was four years old, caused by a gas explosion that had ripped through the block of flats where they were living.

For most of that time she'd sort of believed that her mother was dead too. Auntie Syliva and Uncle Derek had never talked to her much about her real parents. Her dad had been Uncle Derek's brother. About her mother she knew nothing, except that there'd been a huge quarrel between the two families, when Elinor was a baby; and her mother had been the cause. Elinor didn't know what had happened, but she understood that even the terrible accident had changed nothing, in Auntie Sylvia's eyes. Elinor's vanished mother was regarded as a hated enemy, never mentioned except with violent dislike.

It was only recently that she'd discovered the truth.

Elinor touched the burn scar that stretched from her left cheek, down her throat and over her shoulder. It wasn't a terrible scar. It had faded a lot in nearly nine years. On her face it was nearly invisible: the skin was only slightly crumpled, like crêpe paper. She didn't think of it except when her aunt made pitying remarks or Nathalie and Megan teased. But one day at school, a week before the end of this summer term, a boy had asked her how it had happened. It had been at lunchtime. She couldn't remember how or why she'd come to be in the middle of the group, the centre of attention. That wasn't usual. Elinor didn't talk much, or make friends easily.

The boy's name was Ryan. He was in her year but not in her class or he'd probably have heard about Elinor. Nathalie rarely missed a chance to explain that Elinor was a poor relation, not her real sister. But Elinor could tell he wasn't being mean. He was being brave, getting the 'poor thing' factor out into the open, instead of whispering behind her back. The other faces had looked sympathetic, too. So Elinor had told the story of the fire: how her father had been killed, and her friend Emily who was staying overnight with her had been killed, and her pet kitten, and Emily's mother and father in the flat downstairs, and other people too. Elinor had been rescued, but no one had known who she was, because she was unconscious and badly burned. And then she'd had to stay in hospital for ages, and go back for skin-graft operations. Elinor's listeners had become very solemn, listening to the account of this terrible tragedy.

'What about your mother?' Ryan had asked. 'Didn't *she* know who you were?'

'Oh no,' said Elinor, flustered by the attention. 'She wasn't there. My mother died ages ago. Practically before I was born –'

The other children had murmured in sympathy. Somebody sighed: 'You poor thing!'

Ryan had looked shocked. 'Double rough luck! I hope you don't mind talking about it. I didn't mean to upset you –'

Then Nathalie (who was there of course. Elinor could never get away from Nathalie) had laughed and said, 'Don't be daft, Elinor. Your mum's not dead. Elinor's mum ran off with a sailor,' she'd told the whole group. 'Ran off and never came back, not even when her dad died. That's why we have to have her living with us.'

In her refuge under the yew tree Elinor began to tremble as she relived the shame of that moment. She didn't know how she'd survived the rest of that week in school; or how she was going to face Ryan or those other children when she went back in September. She tried to tell herself that everyone would have forgotten. But there was Nathalie. Nathalie and Elinor were almost the same age and always in the same class, so that people who didn't know thought they must be twins. Nathalie wouldn't let anyone forget. Since that day, she'd invented a new anti-Elinor trick. Any time her parents weren't looking she would clasp her hands under her chin, bat her eyelashes and lisp, in a silly whimpering voice: 'My mother died, *pwactically before I was born*!' and then burst into a false, cruel laugh.

Elinor truly remembered her father: his voice, his laugh, his sparkling eyes; the smell of his jacket and the feel of his arms. She did not have any true memories of her mother, only the ones she had constructed – like the police working up an identikit picture of the missing person. She knew that beside her bed in the flat there had been a photograph of a woman with a thin, tanned, smiling face, fair hair tied back and deep dimples in her cheeks. The woman was with a little girl in a vivid green garden: she was tucking a red flower into the little girl's hair. In the flat on Highdown Road, her mother had only been there in the photo . . . but little Elinor had known that Mummy was not dead, she was just for some reason gone, living somewhere else. Elinor remembered now. She supposed she must have known the truth all along. Someone must have told her, at least once. She must have put it out of her mind. Better to have a dead mother than one who didn't care.

Auntie Sylvia had been furious with Nathalie when Elinor came home from school crying that day. It was one of the few occasions that Elinor could remember when Nathalie had actually been told off by her mother. But that was probably, she thought bitterly, because Nathalie had aired an unmentionable family secret, not because she'd hurt Elinor's feelings.

'What made you think your mum was dead?' her aunt had demanded crossly. 'I'm sure no one's ever said that to you. She's alive and well, so far as we know. When they found out who you were, after the fire, the authorities tried to trace her: that's when they contacted your uncle. We did our best to help. But we couldn't track her down. She obviously didn't want to be bothered with you, and that's the end of that.'

Auntie Sylvia's eyes, as she said, '*We did our best,*' had taken on a shifty look that Elinor knew well. Helplessly, she understood that her uncle and aunt had not 'done their best'. Even though it meant giving a home to Elinor, whom she didn't want and didn't love, her aunt had not made much attempt to reunite the hated enemy with her daughter; and Uncle Derek was too lazy to resist her will. But what could Elinor do? She was only a child.

The photo had not survived. Nothing had survived the fire: except Elinor. When she was grown up, she had promised herself, she would search until she knew what had become of her lost mother. Yet though she'd made this promise, she was afraid she'd never have the strength to keep it. Better not to know! It would be so awful if Auntie Sylvia was right.

But she ought to be concentrating on the problems of present reality, not brooding on the past. At the moment she ought to be worrying about the bedrooms in the holiday house. She knew that was what Nathalie and Megan had been discussing as they played on the gravestones. She wasn't sure, because nobody had told her much about the details, but she thought there were three bedrooms between four children. There was also a sofa-bed downstairs. But she knew Auntie Sylvia considered such a makeshift arrangement to be in poor taste. No one would be making a nasty fug by sleeping in one of the living rooms. Obviously two of the children would have to share, and obviously one of the two would be Elinor. But who would be the other? Would the children be allowed to decide? Auntie Sylvia was unpredictable in these situations. Sometimes she didn't care, she'd simply tell them to get on with it. But often she would lose her temper and lay down the law, inevitably choosing to enforce the worst possible settlement of whatever was in dispute. And her temper was fierce. There was no use appealing to Uncle Derek, either. He always refused to get involved.

Their destination was somewhere on the outskirts of this little village, called Breadford, on the edge of the moors. When they finally tracked it down the fun would begin. Elinor well remembered the furious rows last time the sisters had been forced to share a room with the hated outsider, in a holiday hotel. It had been easier when Derek was younger. They just put Elinor in with the baby, and she didn't mind that. But he was five now. He wouldn't be sharing. Most likely Nathalie would have a room of her own and Megan would be in with Elinor. She imagined the nine-year-old getting into all her things, spoiling and breaking them; simply taking anything she wanted. But it would be worth it so long as Nathalie was satisfied. If Nathalie wasn't happy, then there would be hell to pay. And Auntie Sylvia would say, '*Don't whine, Elinor. No wonder they tease you, you have to learn not to be so timid.*' But Elinor couldn't learn. She wasn't an assertive person. She hated fighting or rows of any kind.

Absorbed in her own troubles, she noticed slowly that she could hear a child crying. It sounded like Derek, the way he used to sob in the night when he'd had a bad dream. Elinor had always been the one to comfort him, since she slept the lightest. No child should be left to cry like that! But it couldn't be Derek. He wasn't a baby any more. He didn't need Elinor, he'd joined forces with his sisters. Maybe someone from the village was visiting a grave, and had left their toddler sitting alone in his buggy for too long. 'None of my business,' she told herself. She ought to get back to the others, before they came hunting.

'*There* you are,' said Nathalie accusingly, when Elinor appeared on the path in front of the church. 'What have you been doing?'

'Nothing. Just looking at the old gravestones.'

'Oh really? Tell us what you found, then. What's the oldest date you saw?'

Elinor rubbed her bare arms. It was the end of July and a warm day, but the deep yew shade had chilled her. 'Seventeen eighty-eight,' she said.

'That's nothing,' jeered Megan. '*We* saw one with ten sixty-six.'

Megan was obviously snatching at the one historical date that came into her not very well-informed head. Ten sixty-six was the date when William the Conqueror had invaded England. It was unlikely to be featured on a country gravestone. Elinor didn't point this out. She didn't want any trouble.

Nathalie's eyes narrowed dangerously, as if it was Elinor who'd made the wild impossible claim. 'I don't believe you. Where did you see seventeen eighty-eight?'

It had been on the Revelle tomb under the yew tree. 'I don't know,' she said, protecting her hiding place. 'Somewhere around.'

'Why won't you say where? Mum, make her show us this famous tombstone of hers.'

'Ancient church,' said Uncle Derek in a bored voice, ignoring the friction as usual. 'Tick. Now where's the pub?'

'We have to find the Dower House first,' said Auntie Sylvia firmly. 'Leave the historical research for another time, darlings. Elinor can show you her secrets later. Let's follow the vicar's directions.' As they left the churchyard she looked around with a satisfied smile. 'It certainly is a beautiful location; and the vicar was very nice. Very nice, very select. I'm sure there are some lovely people living here. And only twenty minutes from the motorway.'

Nathalie pulled a face behind her father's back. 'All he thinks about is the pub,' she sneered, in an undertone that was meant to be heard.

Her mother winced, and scowled at Elinor. 'Come *on* Elinor. What are you gawping at?'

She had been looking for the crying child. There was no buggy standing on the path, and nobody seemed to be about. But surely she could still hear that miserable insistent sobbing? It was suddenly as close as if the little boy (she felt that it was a little boy, not a little girl) was next to her, on the other side of a thin wall. Elinor shook her head, to rid herself of the phantom sound. None of the others seemed to hear anything.

Her aunt had left the screen door in the church porch open. She went to close it, to give herself an excuse to peer inside. The church was empty. A hand-written sign on the screen door, in beautiful curly black lettering, said *Please keep this door shut. The swallows fly in, and they're frightened when they can't find the way out.* Nice of someone to care, she thought.

'I was about to do that,' snapped Auntie Sylvia, who liked to think *she* was the one who knew the little details about country life. 'No need for you to take it on yourself, Miss Pushy.'

'Where's Dekkie?' Dekkie was Derek's baby nickname.

'He's in the car.'

Megan pinched Elinor's side. 'I'll tell him you called him Dekkie.'

They climbed into the Espace. Megan told Derek that Elinor had called him by his baby name. Derek, wounded in his five-year-old pride, exploded in noisy rage. Auntie Sylvia leaned over from the front seat to placate him with sweets, but whenever she turned back to face the front, Megan would pinch Derek in the softest place at the back of his knee, making him roar again.

'What's the *matter* with you, darling?' his mother demanded.

'She keeps pinching me!'

'Who?'

The two sisters fixed their little brother with cold eyes. 'Elinor,' declared Derek, who knew what was good for him. Elinor was in the back seat, squashed up against the nearside window by a mass of Madison folding chairs and beach things. She couldn't possibly have reached Derek. Auntie Sylvia heaved an angry sigh. 'For heaven's sake leave him alone, Elinor. Sometimes I wonder. Here we are taking you on a beautiful holiday, when you could be in a foster home. After all we've done for you, can't you even behave?'

They had missed their turning twice. They passed, for the third time, the long white house by the church which was called The Rectory, its porch a mass of yellow roses: and then a pub called The Flying Fish, another pub called The White Hart; a shop that was a post office and a derelict methodist chapel. At last, relative calm having broken out in the back of the car, they left the village through a tract of small, shabby modern housing. Auntie Sylvia sniffed. '*That's not very picturesque*!' Elinor felt her car-sickness coming back. She leaned against the closed window beside her, pressing the travel band against her wrist. The road ran between high hedges. Down a track that lead into woodland she glimpsed a deer that seemed to have been standing, listening in horror to their monstrous approach. It stood for a fleeting moment, and then leapt out of sight. A rambling building among trees went gliding by, just visible over the top of the hedge. It must be the place she had seen from her yew tree corner . . . in a moment it was gone.

'Third on the left,' said Uncle Derek, and swivelled the shiny bulk of the Espace into a tiny lane. Bracken and brambles rattled against the paintwork on either side.

'Are you *sure* this is right?' complained Auntie Sylvia.

'The Dower House. Didn't you see the sign? Like the vicar said. First turn's a track, second lane is the big house, no longer inhabited. The third one leads to the Dower House. This approach could do with improvement. Look at that, there's grass growing down the middle.'

The road levelled out at the bottom of a valley. On one side there were marshy-looking fields, on the other, woodland climbed the bare slopes of the moor. A stream ran by. It was hidden in a ditch, but babbled so loudly that it could be heard above the rumbling engine. Megan and Nathalie were silent, glancing at each other with sour faces. They had their own views about this holiday. They had wanted to go to Florida again. Derek had started listening to a story tape. Elinor woke up, for the first time, to the fact that this was the beginning of a fortnight in the depths of the country, in a magical-sounding old house. There were deer. There might be badgers, foxes, otters. If her life had been different, if she had a real family, she'd be feeling so happy . . . But she didn't like the way this lane didn't go anywhere except to The Dower House. The valley was so narrow. There would be no one else around for miles. It was as if she was being carried, helplessly, into the mouth of a trap.

The house was a disappointment. It stood staring into the lane across a wide well-cropped lawn: a solid, rather ugly building without any olde worlde charm. There was a back wing, closed up and awaiting renovation. The part they were to live in was coated in cream-coloured pebble dash, with green paintwork and a grey slate roof. Apart from the lawn, the 'large garden' was mostly laid out in vegetable beds.

'It's been *modernised*,' hissed Auntie Sylvia, in disgust.

'Well, they said that,' Uncle Derek reminded her, parking the Espace on a big patch of very unromantic gravel by the back porch.

'The agents said *modernised internally*. Hot water and plumbing, central heating. I was not expecting *pebble dash*! And the garden's like an allotment!'

'Bit of a doer-upper,' mused Uncle Derek. 'But it's a good new slate roof, none of that messy thatch. That's a plus.'

Auntie Sylvia wanted to move out and live in the country full time. Uncle Derek humoured her by chatting about the subject, but he and the children weren't keen. Elinor knew that this holiday was partly meant as an exploration of the idea: but it didn't seem any of her business.

'I *knew* we should have insisted on photographs.'

They'd collected the keys from the estate agent, in the small market town they'd passed through after leaving the motorway. Everyone climbed out of the car. Auntie Sylvia unlocked the back door and entered her new domain, sniffing suspiciously. Nathalie and Megan quickly vanished, with little Derek hurrying after them.

The modern kitchen was a cold, bare little room that must have been the scullery in the original house. The big old kitchen beyond was now a sort of hybrid, with a glossy aga that didn't look as if it had ever been lit; a dining table and sideboards. Next door on one side there was the study with the sofa-bed, an ice-cold tomb; and on the other a large, chintzy living room with broad low windows that overlooked the lawn. Auntie Sylvia's mood improved. 'Very nice,' she decided, admiring the warming pan that hung above the living room hearth, the harness brasses and the glossy fire-irons. She quickly tested the texture of a chinese fireside rug. 'Mmm, quite new and good quality.' She pressed the cushions of the plump, glossy sofa. 'Nice material. Quite up-market.'

Elinor, who liked old things, found the inside of the house even more disappointing than the outside. The bright rooms felt unlived-in, in some terminal way, and colder than the yew tree's shade. There were far too many knicknacks, in cabinets on the walls and clustered on little tables. It was almost as if someone had tried hard to hide the house's real nature: but something harsh and comfortless managed to defeat all their efforts.

Uncle Derek was relieved at his wife's approval. 'All hands to unload,' he suggested heartily.

Nathalie and Megan's footsteps could be heard overhead: Nathalie's light and sharp, Megan thumping like a baby rhino. There were clambering noises from the stairway, and Derek could be heard yelling, 'Wait for me! I want to explore too!' Elinor was the only 'hand' in sight. Her uncle shrugged. 'Well, get a move on, Elinor. You don't expect your aunt to do all the work, I hope.'

When she was hauling her aunt and uncle's suitcases upstairs, Elinor saw Nathalie and Megan in the first bedroom she came to. They were lying on the twin beds, Nathalie by the window and Megan near the door, chatting. They stopped talking as Elinor went by, and stared in hard, secret silence, bursting into giggles as soon as her back was turned. She located the master bedroom, with the fanciest fittings and the second bathroom en-suite, and put Uncle Derek's and Auntie Sylvia's bags in there. There was also the other bathroom and a small bedroom that held a pair of bunk beds. It had a nice little window-seat, overlooking the lane and the stream. Derek was in there, playing at obstacle courses with a china cat and several carved Indian figures of animals, which he'd taken from a shelf in the upstairs hall. The Dower House, Elinor noted, was not well prepared for a busy-fingered five-year-old. She found a door that led to the closed part of the house, but no third bedroom for the children. It looked as if Megan and Nathalie had decided to share, and she would be with Derek. That was okay. It would be harder now than when he was a baby, but a million times better than being with Megan. She left Nathalie and Megan's bags outside their door, and looked for another task. It would be a good idea to put the most fragile ornaments out of harm's way: now, before there were any disasters.

Auntie Sylvia was inspecting kitchen cupboards, and didn't look round as Elinor passed her. In the big front room, her uncle had settled with beer and peanuts, reading his paper. Elinor showed him the breakables she'd collected. 'Where can I put these? I thought I'd move them out of Dekkie's way.'

Uncle Derek reached for his beer. 'Right. It's ridiculous, leaving fiddly little antiques around in a holiday home. Put them anywhere you like, so long as it's out of the way.'

With a vague gesture towards the fireplace, he vanished behind his newspaper. There was a door in that direction, but she knew that it was locked, and there was no key for it on the key ring they'd picked up from the estate agents. That was one of the features of the Dower House, as she had already discovered. There seemed to be more doors than there were rooms. She went out into the hall again, and counted. One door for the study, one for the big kitchen with the aga (you had to go through there to get to the back kitchen), one for the living room . . . and one more. Of course it was locked. She put her armful of ornaments down and looked around; and then, just on the off-chance, reached up and ran her hand along the ledge at the top of the low, old fashioned door frame. Something rattled and fell. She had found the key!

It was big and old and dusty; but it turned all right. She opened the door: she was looking into the closed-off wing of the Dower House. There was a hallway, facing the original front entrance of the house. A flight of stairs, grander than the ones from the kitchen, must lead to the shut-off rooms on the upper floor. There was a faint musty smell. The inevitable ornaments looked shabbier, and more real. A moth-eaten fox, killing a withered rabbit among ornamental everlasting grasses, stood in a glass box on the hall stand. There was an elephant's foot made into a holder for walking sticks, something she had often heard of but had never seen.

Elinor felt that she'd found the real Dower House, and it was a much more interesting place. Briefly, she let herself imagine that things were different. If she was *really* part of this family, presumably she'd have been lying upstairs idle, chatting with her sisters. But maybe not. She was the oldest. Maybe she was the responsible one, the daughter Auntie Sylvia could trust. The door on her right must be the locked one by the front room fireplace. What about the one on her left? Warmed by her aunt's imaginary approval she put the breakables down again and turned the key that stood in yet another big old-fashioned lock. There was a short passage on the other side. It had no windows, so it was very dark. She could hardly make out the colour of the door at the end.

'Oh no,' whispered Elinor. She did not like being shut in; and this dark passage seemed narrow as a grave. She put her hand to her throat, feeling as if she couldn't breathe. But she had to learn to be less timid. She searched and found an iron doorstop in the shape of a cow, lurking behind the elephant's foot. That was better. With the door propped open, light and an escape route behind, she made it to the other end. There was another stiff old-fashioned lock. So many locked doors! 'This house is ridiculous,' she muttered, as she struggled to turn it, juggling with her burden of sharp-edged curios and slippery china. She managed to get inside the room and plonk everything down on a flat surface before anything disastrous happened: and then she looked around.

The walls of the room were panelled in wood. Two stiff-backed chairs with embroidered seats stood on either side of the fireplace, two black carved oak chests stood against the walls. There was a washstand with a big old-fashioned jug and basin, a battered walnut desk; and in the centre of the room stood a fourposter bed, complete with canopy and curtains. The air was stale, the ancient furniture was shabby, and everything was thinly coated in dust. She was puzzled to see that it was arranged as a bedroom. Surely that couldn't have been its original purpose? But that wasn't what worried her. It was *that bed.* It looked, as old fourposters do, as if it was too short for a normal person. It looked like a musty trap, a prison that would close in on you in the night.

Elinor had had enough. She left, making sure that all three doors were locked behind her.

In the kitchen Auntie Sylvia was muttering to herself as she made her inventory. 'No salad bowl. There must be a salad bowl. Ah, here it is. Cheap and nasty. Nice gravy boat, though. Just like one we used to have.'

Elinor discovered that she wanted to get out of the Dower House, even if it was only for a few minutes. She was surprised at how much the fourposter room had bothered her. It was spooky but it was locked away. There were worse things to fear. But she couldn't get past her aunt to reach the scullery porch.

'Auntie Sylvia, what shall I do with the key to the back wing?'

'What a horrible little toaster, and that crumb-tray hasn't been cleaned for years.'

'I think it ought to be locked, it leads to the part we're not to use.'

Her aunt looked up, with an annoyed expression. 'Elinor, how many times have I told you: *don't call me "Auntie"*. It sounds so common.'

Somehow no one had ever thought that Elinor should call her aunt and uncle Mum and Dad. Nathalie wouldn't have liked it, anyway.

'I'm sorry, Aunt Sylvia. But where shall I put it? I've hidden the worst breakables, the things Uncle Derek thought should be kept out of Dekkie's way, in the downstairs bedroom off the front hall. I found the key on top of the door. Shall I put it back there?'

'What are you talking about?'

'The . . . the rooms we're not to use. I've locked the door again.'

Auntie Sylvia had fixed on something else. 'What do you mean "breakables"? Our Derek isn't going to break anything. He's a very careful, gentle little boy. There's no reason to strip the place. At the rent we're paying! If you've put things away, you can fetch them back, you cheeky girl. Anyway, there is no "downstairs bedroom".'

'Y-yes there is.'

Auntie Sylvia suddenly looked interested. 'You'd better show me.'

So Elinor, still trying to be helpful and useful, opened the low door in the hall again, and led Auntie Sylvia into the closed-off wing. Her aunt gazed, speculatively, at the broad staircase, and the spacious front hallway. She was less impressed by the room at the end of the narrow passage. 'Hmmph,' she said, 'looks like an old furniture dump.' She didn't seem affected by the atmosphere. But she went over and poked the mattress of the bed: and a light dawned in her eyes. 'Well, this does solve a problem. You can sleep in here, Elinor.'

'But we're not supposed to use this part of the house,' quavered Elinor. 'It was locked.'

'At the rent we're paying? Nonsense.' Aunt Sylvia looked triumphant. 'We rented the house, and that means the whole thing, as far as I'm concerned. I always did think that was a cheeky arrangement. I was going to put you on the camp-bed which is supposed to be somewhere about, in with Nathalie and Megan. But I know the girls didn't like the idea. This is much better all round. Now fetch your bag, which I noticed you've left in Dekkie's room when I went upstairs just now: get yourself unpacked and come and help me with the tea. I mean the dinner. And stop answering back!'

Elinor bit her lip. She knew she was in danger of a hard slap. Auntie Sylvia was never reluctant to use her hands when she was angry. She didn't know what was making her so reckless, but she could not believe in her fate.

'I thought I'd better share with Derek. In case he gets nightmares –'

'You're too old to share with a little boy. It wouldn't be nice. If he has a bad dream, he'll want his mummy. Oh, and another thing, Miss Pushy, I suppose you plan to lie there in state, surrounded by all the prettiest *objets* in the house. Well, you have another think coming. You put the ornaments back where you found them *at once.* And leave Dekkie alone!'

Aunt Sylvia had a habit of getting at Elinor, usually when her own children had let her down by being rude or refusing to help with the chores. It didn't mean much. It wasn't as bad as a slap. Elinor tried not to let it bother her.

'I could have the sofa-bed in the study.'

'*Stop talking nonsense.* I told you before, I will not have smelly bedclothes around in our living rooms. What's got into you? Get your bag, and be quick!'

She hurried up the stairs. Derek was still playing his obstacle game. He'd taken some small things from Elinor's bag to replace the breakables she'd rescued.

'Derek, sweetheart, I'm going to share with you, aren't I? I'll play with you as much as you like, and I'll read to you, and be here when you have a bad dream.'

The little boy glanced up, with a sly smile. 'No,' he said. 'You belong down-below stairs.'

'I'll let you have the top bunk –'

'No. You can't.'

He was repeating what he'd been told to say, and Elinor had been out-manoeuvred. Someone sniggered. She turned and saw Nathalie and Megan, arm in arm, grinning in the doorway of their room. They burst into peals of laughter.

'We're none of us going to share with you,' declared Nathalie. 'We don't care how Mum sorts you out. You can sleep in the study, or in the garage for all we care.'

Derek dragged Elinor's unzipped bag from off the bottom bunk. He shoved it out into the passage, and kicked the rest of her possessions after it.

'*Down-below stairs*!' he roared.

'*We're the real Madisons! We're the real Madisons!*' chanted Nathalie and Megan, with vicious glee . . .

Derek had changed as he grew from a toddler into a child. You could see that he was going to be chunky like Megan, not slim and elegant like Nathalie. He was going to look like his father. Suddenly Elinor finally, absolutely realised that the baby boy she had loved was gone forever. She felt hot with rage, to think that she had *pleaded* with the little monster. But rage never worked for her. It came out as pathetic, feeble tears. She pushed her jumbled things back into the bag, trying to hide the stinging drops that fell on to her cheeks, and slunk off downstairs while her cousins stood and laughed.

She tried to tell herself that there was nothing wrong with the room. The oak-panelled walls were dark, but they were beautifully made and carved. The furniture was very old and interesting. She thought the chests and the bed were seventeenth century, the desk and chairs maybe a hundred years younger. It was a privilege to be allowed to use such things: full of history, full of hundreds of years of human life. She just wished she didn't have to sleep in that bed. It was too far off the ground. The mattress, which was covered by a swollen, glistening pall of eiderdown, was too thick and it smelled of mothballs. The heavy curtains felt cold and rough as stone, the canopy was like a coffin lid.

She wished she hadn't thought of that.

She tried to put the word 'coffin' out of her mind, and found some clean blankets in one of the chests. She would have to keep her clothes in the other, which was empty, since there was no ordinary chest of drawers or wardrobe. She made up her bed with Madison sheets and Dower House blankets, but without the eiderdown; which was so heavy it would be like sleeping under a rock. She wrestled the slippery monster into some kind of folds and bundled it into the blanket chest. Then she unpacked the rest of her things. On her knees in front of the other chest, she peered at the old newspapers that lined it. They were pages from something called *The Western Advertiser*, June 1975.

The house felt very silent. Her cousins, even Nathalie, were probably asleep. Auntie Sylvia and Uncle Derek would be watching videos in bed, as was their custom. They'd brought the TV and VCR from their bedroom at home, having been warned that reception down here was tricky. But not a sound reached Elinor. It was as if the bright, fake country-life rented rooms had ceased to exist out there; and the past had come flooding back. The old house, the Dower House, standing silent and empty; alone in the narrow valley between the moors.

It had been a long evening. Nathalie and Megan had been in foul tempers because they weren't allowed to watch television. Their parents' TV was for the grown-ups' exclusive use. Auntie Sylvia wanted her children to enjoy more refined entertainment. So they'd been forced to play Scrabble with their cousin, which was not much fun for Elinor. But she had endured without complaint, even when Megan knocked everyone's tiles over, and Nathalie took the opportunity to swop her bad letters for Elinor's good ones. She had made up her mind to *fight back*, this time: but quietly, secretly, the way that suited her. It was the expression on Dekkie's face that had made her brave. She would not be despised by the baby who had been her playmate and her comfort. So the tears had stopped. She was not going to show them that she was afraid of sleeping in the spooky room. For the rest of this fortnight there would be no trembling, no pleading for mercy. That spooky room would be a test of her resolution to be strong: and she already had the satisfaction of knowing that Nathalie and Megan *knew* something had changed. They'd been disappointed of their usual fun this evening. That's what had made them so angry, more than missing the TV.

Elinor had washed and brushed her teeth in the tiny 'cloakroom' off the scullery. (Auntie Sylvia had pointed out how convenient this was for the 'downstairs bedroom', causing Nathalie and Megan to snigger again about Elinor living in the servants' quarters). She hoped she wouldn't need the toilet in the night. It would be an unpleasant journey. She changed into her pyjamas and stood in front of the oval mirror that hung on the wall. Elinor's hair was light brown instead of chestnut and her eyes were grey instead of blue, but she was enough like her cousins to be stamped with their identity – like a diluted Madison, as if she was an extra child made up from the same pattern with not quite so much material. You had to study her face carefully to see that it was a different shape, and her complexion a different tone: and nobody paid that much attention to Elinor.

She wished that she could believe that she looked like her lost mother. But when she tried to compare herself with that dimly-remembered photo, she couldn't be sure. It was better not to think about such things, she only made herself more miserable.

'Poor relation!' she told herself bitterly. 'That's what you look like, that's what you are.'

Maybe it would have been different if she was different: more bold and boisterous, able to stand up for herself. Maybe she'd have fitted in. But she couldn't change her personality, and anyway she didn't *want* to. The Madisons didn't want her, and she didn't want them. It would have been better if she'd had no relations. Then she might have had a chance to get adopted after Daddy died, and find a new family of her own.

The room's cold atmosphere weighed on her soul. She braided up her hair, and grimly climbed into the fourposter. She expected it would be incredibly hard to get to sleep. But she was really very tired . . .

She'd been sleeping for a long time, so long that she thought it must be morning, when she woke up *knowing* that somebody had come into the room. It had to be Nathalie. Nathalie had crept down here and was going through Elinor's belongings. She must be either looking for something, or else planting something to get Elinor into trouble. Nathalie had once kicked up a tremendous fuss about a new black sweater, which had vanished (she said) from her clothes cupboard. The whole house had been turned upside down and the sweater had been found hidden away in Elinor's chest of drawers. Elinor was certain that Nathalie had put it there herself. But of course she couldn't prove that and she'd had to take the blame.

She opened her eyes without moving, hoping to catch her cousin in the act (not that it would do her any good. Auntie Sylvia believed any tale the cousins told against Elinor, no matter whether it made sense). It wasn't morning. It was still night, and although she'd left the curtains at her window open, the room was dark the way no night ever is in a town. But there was a kind of glow around a figure seated in front of the walnut desk, its back to Elinor. It was the figure of a woman with a big, nodding pile of whitish hair, and a sort of train fastened to her shoulders. She seemed to be searching the desk, opening all the little drawers jerkily and fast. Something, anyway, caused the pleated robe that hung from her shoulders to move, so that the patterned silk glittered in the light that came from nowhere.

Elinor lay very still and deadly cold. It was a dream, of course: one of those dreams where you're scared to death by something that seems outwardly quite harmless. She remembered once waking in terror, waking the whole house with her screams; and all she could tell them, when her aunt and uncle came running, was: *The red ball! The red ball! It's bouncing!* And they had been very angry. This was the same. She was going to wake up soon, because when you know a dream's a dream its power is broken.

Let me wake up! Let me wake up! Please!

The figure at the writing desk stood, and looked towards the fourposter bed with such a face: with such ghastly white, sunken cheeks and such dread and horror in its eyes . . . It crossed the room. Something like flames seemed to flicker around its gliding skirts. It disappeared. Elinor sat bolt upright, screaming and screaming.

She had wakened herself, and there was no one in the room. There wasn't a sound from the rest of the house. Either nobody had heard her screams, or she had only dreamed that she was screaming. She lay down again, her heart still pounding. 'Thank goodness that's over,' she whispered. She reached to switch on her light. There wasn't a bedside table or cabinet in the room so she'd moved one of the chairs, and balanced the lamp that had been standing on top of the desk (a handsome lamp with a base in the shape of a bronze dragon) on the seat. The arrangement wasn't very secure, she'd been afraid it wouldn't work. Sure enough, the lamp seemed to have slipped from the chair. She groped, but could not find it. The curtains of the fourposter bed – of course Elinor had not closed them – were looped back and tied with heavy gilt cord at each of the four posts. As she fumbled, she somehow loosened the fastenings. With a horrible soft rushing sound the curtains fell around her. The country darkness of the room turned to utter, smothering black. The canopy overhead pressed down on her, it was as if she was lying in a grave. She was buried alive, the bed was her tomb, and in a moment the old woman with the horrible face would part the hangings and look in.

She tried to scream and couldn't. The blankets were heavy as lead, the earth lay on her face, the fourposter bed was her tomb, *she was buried alive* . . .

How long her paralysed terror lasted, Elinor didn't know. It could have been years, it could have been no time at all. Frantically, she dived out from under the covers and fell on to the floor, hurting her knee. She righted her lamp – luckily the bulb hadn't broken – and switched it on. She discovered, of course, that the bed curtains hadn't fallen down. The big knots in those cords couldn't come undone, they hadn't been touched for years. She climbed on to the bed again and crouched there with her head in her hands. What a horrible dream! But there was no point in crying. There was nothing to be done except try to get back to sleep.

She lay for a long time in misery, afraid to sleep and afraid to have the light on. There'd been big trouble once when her aunt had caught her reading late at night; and she was not feeling lucky. Then, as her thoughts were growing muddled and blurred at last, she seemed to hear the door of her room softly opening. Soft footsteps, a *child's* footsteps came pattering towards the bed. Fear rushed through her, a feeling of horror and terror worse than anything that had gone before . . .

She could hear the little boy's quick, sobbing breath. He'd been crying. He had come to her for comfort, of course. Her terror vanished. Why had she been afraid?

'Dekkie?' she whispered gently. 'Is that you? Did you have a bad dream?'

Without a word he scrambled up and burrowed under the bedclothes. He was trembling. 'Don't be frightened,' murmured Elinor, hugging him. 'I'm here. Do you want to say what the dream was?' A shake of the head that was pressed against her shoulder. 'Okay, never mind. We're still friends, are we? I'm glad. You can stay with me till morning.' She fell asleep, wonderfully comforted.

Derek was gone when she woke up. By the time Elinor ventured into the Madisons' part of the house for breakfast he'd reverted to normal. When she was stupid enough to ask if he'd got over his nightmare, the little boy was furious. Elinor had to back off at once, and she wondered if the whole thing had been a dream, the nightmare and the comforting part as well.

Two

FOR A WHILE THE WEATHER WAS KIND AND THE holiday was successful. They had come to the depths of the country, but luckily the bustling seaside was not far away. Every morning after breakfast the Espace sailed forth, laden with bicycles, folding loungers, radio, mobile phone, towels and picnic food. Auntie Sylvia grumbled a little about her children's preference for the beach above classier pleasures, but otherwise there wasn't a cloud in the Madisons' sky.

These days were not exactly ideal for Elinor. She was the one who had to wash up quickly after breakfast and hurriedly make the sandwiches. On the beach she had the job of looking after Derek – who hated her because he wanted to trail after his sisters. And she couldn't swim. The T-shirt her aunt insisted she had to wear so her scar wouldn't show made her self-conscious, so she didn't like to go in the water anyway. As they crawled in holiday traffic-jams, she would look out at the great moorland: the rock formations like basking whales, the seas of green bracken and surf of white bog-cotton, and wished she could plunge into that different ocean of sun and air. But on the whole it wasn't too bad. She'd known worse. She could survive as long as Nathalie and Megan were having a good time.

Her nights too were not pleasant, but they were tolerable. She had cleaned the fourposter room. Nothing could lighten the room's stale, cold atmosphere: she couldn't open the windows, which were swollen shut from years of damp. But it was better without the dust. She had secured some candles and matches to keep by her bed, and slept with her door ajar. Sometimes she was forced to get up five or six times before she could relax, to check that the door at the end of the passage (so narrow, and dark as the grave) was open too, and safely held back by the iron cow doorstop. The bed curtains were the worst part. She had to check those knots time and again, and still she would lie awake convinced that they were about to close, trapping her in their stifling folds. But she didn't have the nightmare about the horrible old lady again, though she often woke with the certainty that someone was in the room. And she was still fighting back. When her cousins laughed at her for having to wash in the scullery; when they called her the servant who had to sleep 'below-stairs' she didn't say anything. Sometimes she allowed herself a little smile. She had a faint hope that Nathalie would start thinking she was missing something, and insist on a room swop.

Then one day it rained. The family woke to a steady downpour, and the forecast on the radio promised more of the same. The Madison children were bad-tempered, and squabbled over the choice of a rainy-day tourist attraction. Uncle Derek couldn't stand this sort of thing. He called his office and discovered that he ought to go in for an hour or so to sort a few things out. They'd left his business car at home so he drove off in the Espace, promising to be back by lunchtime. He regularly did this on holiday. When he'd had enough of his children (which didn't take long), he would simply disappear. But this time, as everyone realised too late, he had actually left them stranded, with no transport. Auntie Sylvia was furious. She retired to the cold study, and sat there smoking cigarettes – a bad sign, as she'd been successfully off them since Christmas.

Elinor had been praying for rain. The village was only half a mile away. She could go out by herself and visit her yew tree. She washed up after breakfast, tidied the kitchen, had her shower and cleaned the upstairs bathroom, which was in a mess. Then she put on her waterproof and tried to slip out of the back door. But as she struggled with the bolt, Auntie Sylvia burst into the back kitchen.

'Where do you think you're going?' she demanded.

'Just out for a bit of a walk.'

'Oh no, you don't. Get back in the front room and play with your cousins, Miss Thinks-She's-Too-Good-For-Us. Wait for your uncle. We're going out today *as a family*.'

By two o'clock Uncle Derek hadn't returned. Nathalie and Megan were grumbling over a jigsaw. Derek was playing with his cars. Elinor sat in the window, staring out at the streaming rain. She could not read because her head ached. She never woke rested after a night in the fourposter room. Sleeping in there was more like a struggle that left you exhausted. How she longed to be alone in the green wet world outside . . . Suddenly something hit her on the cheek. She looked round, startled. A jigsaw piece was lying on the carpet at her feet.

Megan sniggered. 'Pick it up,' ordered Nathalie.

The sisters were grinning, elbows on the card table in a drift of jigsaw fragments. Megan threw another piece. It landed in Elinor's lap. 'Pick it up!' she jeered.

Elinor, impelled by reckless weariness, brushed it on to the floor, and turned her back on them.

More pieces showered.

'Pick them up! Pick them up, servant-girl!'

The attack was senseless, but it wasn't funny. When they were in this mood they'd do anything. She knew she had to get out of their sight.

'You're crazy,' she said: stood up and walked away.

She went to the fourposter room, because there was nowhere else. She couldn't find the cow doorstop, but it was daylight and she managed to brave the passage. As soon as she walked into the room the atmosphere descended on her, as strong as ever. A horror was always waiting here: something deathly and old and wicked. She had grown almost used to it at night, but in daylight the shock was as real as the first time.

Then she noticed that things had been moved. The hateful eiderdown, which had been stuffed inside the blanket chest, was in a heap on top of it. Elinor's hairbrush had vanished. The drawer in the wash-stand, where she kept her candle and matches, was open: and it was empty. For a moment, the hairs on the back of her neck stood on end. Then she realised, of course, her cousins had been in here. The most terrible idea struck her. She leapt for the door. She was right. The key, which she had left in the lock, had gone. There was no key in the door at the other end of the passage, either. And the doorstop, too. They had even taken the doorstop!

She knew what they had meant to do. They had meant to wait until Elinor was in bed, and then come down and lock her in. They knew how terrified she was of confined spaces, of being trapped. They had wanted her to be *shut in here in the night*, in that vile fourposter bed, *knowing that she would scream and scream, and no one would come, because even if her aunt or uncle heard her, they'd ignore it. Just Elinor making a silly fuss . . .* Elinor felt so angry and horrified that she was nearly sick. She ran back into the front room.

'Give me the keys!' she yelled.

'What keys?' smirked Megan.

'*The key to my room. And to the door in the hall.* You took them this morning, didn't you, when I was cleaning up the bathroom –'

'It isn't *your* room,' drawled Nathalie, pretending to look for a piece in the jigsaw box. '*Our* parents rented this house. You are only here because we keep you out of charity.'

'I don't see what's specially charitable about it. I'm your *cousin*. In any normal family, that would mean something. I wouldn't be treated like a – like a servant!'

'Cinder-Elinor!' chanted Megan, in delight. 'Cinder-Elinor!'

Nathalie linked her fingers under her chin, in a fake winsome pose. '*My mammy died pwactically before I was born!*' she lisped. Megan quickly copied her. They chanted in chorus: '*Pwactically before I was born! Pwactically before I was born!*'

They looked so *happy*. That was what finally made Elinor snap.

She had never struck out at her cousins, or anybody else, before in her life. She launched herself at them, trying to hit them both at once, clawing and punching at those unbearably smug, joyful faces. The folding card table crashed over on its side, legs splayed. Jigsaw pieces scattered. Megan began to scream, '*Mum!* Elinor's gone mad! She's killing Nathalie!'

Elinor and Nathalie rolled on the floor, kicking and struggling. Derek came running over and started to hit Elinor around the head with one of his metal cars –

'WHAT IS GOING ON????'

Two hard and angry hands grabbed Elinor by the shoulders and pulled her to her feet. Nathalie got up and stood breathing hard. Auntie Sylvia turned Elinor round. Elinor had a moment of staring, too close, into her aunt's furious face, then she was shoved backwards into the nearest chair.

'My God. You've broken the card table. We're going to have to replace that. It'll probably cost the earth. WHAT WAS ALL THAT ABOUT???'

Nathalie touched a scratch on her cheek, looked at a tiny streak of blood on her fingertip and shuddered dramatically. 'I don't really know,' she said, in a low, trembling voice.

'She went mad!' broke in Megan excitedly.

'Elinor had taken candles and matches from the kitchen and was keeping them in her room,' said Nathalie. 'I thought that wasn't safe, so I moved them –'

'Quite right, good girl,' nodded Auntie Sylvia, staring at Elinor in disgust.

'I don't know why, but that seemed to make Elinor furious. She – she leapt at me.'

'She shouldn't have been in my room!' cried Elinor. 'She's taken my keys!'

'Oh, yes, I took the keys, too, Mum. I thought, if she was going to be irresponsible like that she shouldn't be able to shut herself in. It would be dangerous.'

'She said we treated her like a servant!' piped up Megan.

Nathalie closed her eyes. 'I think I'm going to faint,' she whispered.

Auntie Sylvia put her arms around her older daughter. 'All right, love, calm down. Let me get something for that cut.' Nathalie murmured 'Thank you.' Moaning a little, she laid her cheek, the unscratched one, against her mother's shoulder. Derek, scowling at Elinor, held Nathalie's hand. Megan, her round eyes bright with pleasure, ostentatiously began to pick up jigsaw pieces.

'And *you*,' snarled Auntie Sylvia, 'you can go to your room, and stay there. Like a servant, eh? You cheeky little . . .' She was lost for words bad enough. 'We'll see what your uncle has to say about this when he gets home.'

Elinor had cracked her head hard on a corner of the fireplace. She was dizzy, and everything seemed far away. Her aunt took her by the arm, marched her to the fourposter room and shut her in. She didn't resist. Minutes later she heard footsteps again, and the key turned in the lock. She wondered what was the worst that could be done to her. She could be put into care, as being *beyond parental control.* That was a threat she had often heard. Usually it had no foundation, it was just one of the things Auntie Sylvia said when she was in a temper. Elinor was far too timid to be naughty. She had certainly never hit Nathalie before. So maybe this time it would happen. She would be sent away. She wondered if being put in 'a home' could be worse than what she had to bear already.

She sat on the floor, numbly unwilling to sit on the bed or on one of those stiff chairs: and waited, in a daze. Before long the Espace came rumbling down the lane. She heard it turn and park on the gravel. Soon she would know her fate.

Nothing happened.

At last she heard chatter out of doors. Dimly, from the other side of the house, she heard the usual loud performance of getting everybody into the car. 'Come on, come on, we don't want to miss the main feature! *Nathalie, we're waiting for you!*' Doors slammed. The engine started up, the Espace drove away.

They had gone out and left her.

Maybe it was a trick. They would turn back and come and fetch her, satisfied that she'd been frightened enough. But no one came.

'Now I am alone,' whispered Elinor.

When she realised that nobody was going to come back for her, she seriously decided to run away. The fourposter room was on the ground floor. She knew the windows wouldn't open but she could *break* one and climb out, taking what possessions she could carry. She had enough money for a bus to the nearest big town. She would live on the streets, sleep in doorways. But she didn't have the courage. You have to feel positive about something before you can run away, if it's only about being desperate. Elinor didn't have that kind of spirit.

She rocked herself to and fro, hating her own helplessness. But she had reached some kind of breaking point. 'I'll do *something*,' she whispered to herself. 'I'm going to get back at them. *I swear it*.'

A trickle of blood had dried on her cheek. There was a swelling bump on her temple where she'd struck her head on the fireplace, but the blood came from a cut behind her ear, where Derek had been hitting her with his car. When she touched the place to find out how badly she was cut it started to bleed again: and that gave her an idea. *I will curse them*, she thought.

She looked for something to write on. She didn't have a notebook and she didn't keep a diary (her cousins or her aunt would have found it and read it. What's the point in keeping a diary that's read by your tormenters?). She tore a slip of paper from the front of *Swallowdale*, one of the paperbacks she'd brought with her, and prepared to lay a curse on the Madisons. A used match from the washstand drawer, the clean end roughly sharpened, made a kind of pen. She squeezed the cut ruthlessly, until she'd managed to collect a tiny pool of blood on the rim of the washstand bowl.

What should she write? It would have to be short. Their names, first.

Nathalie, she wrote. *Megan*: and then hesitated. Dekkie! That hurt the most. Elinor could understand why Nathalie hated her. She could see it must be hard to be forced to share your mum and dad with an outsider. And she could see why Megan was bound to follow Nathalie's lead. But Elinor had *loved* Derek. She had comforted him, cuddled him and played with him. How could he turn on her? He was as bad as his sisters. No, he was worse. She dipped the matchstick again in her own blood, and formed the name: *Dekkie.*

Nathalie, Megan, Dekkie

Underneath, she wrote:

Harm to them.

Some of the letters were mere smears, others just scratches. But the message was clear enough. Now what should she do? She should pierce the charm with magic thorns, seal it with wax, burn it on a fire of potent herbs; or maybe bury it in a graveyard at full moon. Since she couldn't do anything like that, she decided to hide it somewhere secure. She looked around. Nathalie and Megan had been through this room once, they could do it again. The washstand was too obvious and so were the chests. She turned to the walnut desk. The memory of her nightmare hung about it like an invisible shroud. But today things were different. She drew a chair across and sat down. It had once been a beautiful piece of furniture. The top was damaged and one foot had been clumsily repaired: but Elinor, who loved old things, could see its quality. She opened the outer drawers, one by one. They were all empty, and smelling faintly of some smoky perfume. She tried the doors of the recessed cabinet above the writing surface. They weren't locked. Inside she found two more stacks of smaller drawers, and soon discovered that the third one down on the left was half the length it should be. When you pulled it out a false back was revealed. This was just what she had been expecting. She tugged gently and the hinged panel came away, revealing a secret compartment. Of course there was nothing in it.

'That'll do,' muttered Elinor. She was sure her cousins wouldn't get this far. They didn't read the kind of books Elinor read, and they knew nothing about antique furniture. But as she reached for her charm, which was lying tightly folded on the writing space, her elbow knocked the left-hand cabinet door. She heard something move, inside the thickness of the wood. Intrigued, she examined the door closely and found a tiny button on the underside. When she pressed it a slim block slipped down, smoothly, as if it had been set into place yesterday. She had found another hidey-hole, more secret than the first. But this one wasn't empty. When she felt inside, a soft packet dropped into her hand. It was a little purse of withered chamois leather. Inside, there was a pair of earrings.

They were long and dangly, each of them a lyre-shaped frame of silver, hung with filigree drops and warm golden stones. As soon as she touched the stones Elinor knew that they were amber. The two largest, one set in the centre of each lyre frame, were matched teardrop-shapes as big as Elinor's thumb-nail and the colour of honey. Each held a tiny fly, suspended. The silver was tarnished black, but it was exquisitely worked. She rubbed at the lyre frames, and made out the shapes of little winged things, flies and bees and moths. Flies in amber, bugs in silver: someone had peculiar taste.

'They must belong to someone,' she told herself. 'They belong to the owner of the Dower House.' But her hand had closed over the earrings, as if all by itself. They were weird, but they were lovely and alluring. Already, she wanted them more than anything. *Nobody knew they were here*, she thought. *Nobody will know if I keep them.*

Perhaps that's what the old lady in the dream had been doing. Perhaps she had been searching for these earrings, a lost treasure. Elinor shuddered at the idea, because there was something blighted about these jewels, although they were so desirable. She remembered the terrible face of the old lady: and knew, very strongly, that the earrings were guilty things. Somehow they were to blame for the horrible atmosphere in this room. But still . . . she wanted them. Then another thought came to her, from nowhere: a frightening one. If she stole these wicked earrings, then the spell she had made to do her cousins harm would come true. She was sure of this. She was being offered a bargain: evil for evil.

'That's stupid,' declared Elinor, aloud: and she held the earrings tightly, as if someone was trying to take them away. 'Anyway, they're not exactly treasure. Silver's cheap, and the amber's probably fake. I bet the last holiday-makers left them behind. I expect they're not very old, and worth about two pounds fifty.'

She didn't let herself think any more. She hid the folded paper where the earrings had been, and closed up the desk. Then she hid the earrings, in their leather purse, under the mattress of the fourposter bed. A few minutes ago she hadn't considered the fourposter as a hiding place, because she was afraid of it. But that seemed silly now. She knelt on the rug by the empty hearth, chilled and shaky and yet triumphant. '*Something bad's going to happen*,' she whispered, defiantly. '*They'll be sorry.*'

Three

THE WEATHER HAD CHANGED AGAIN. IT WAS GOING to be one of the hottest days of the year, and Auntie Sylvia, in one of her rare, doomed attempts at parent power, had decreed that they were finally going to do some sightseeing. Elinor had been sent to the village baker's to fetch fresh bread and cakes for a moorland picnic. But she'd been quick, and she thought she could afford to visit the churchyard.

When the Madisons had returned from the cinema that day, Auntie Sylvia had come at once and unlocked the door of Elinor's room. By then Elinor had been lying on the hearthrug, quietly reading. Her aunt had said something like, 'I hope you've learned your lesson,' and that had been it. There had been no telling off, not a word from her uncle. Her terrible crimes had been forgotten. She suspected that Auntie Sylvia felt she'd gone too far by leaving Elinor locked up alone for all that time.

Since then, Elinor had as usual taken the brunt of the chores, and endured her cousins' bullying and her aunt's bad temper. But nothing worse had happened. She felt confident enough to snatch a few moments of freedom. She left her bicycle at the gate and walked among the graves, where wild flowers were fading in the uncut grass. A man in grubby blue overalls was up on a ladder against the wall of the nave, clearing out a gutter. Elinor tried to get by unnoticed, but he called cheerfully, 'Hello. Have you come to see the church? Sorry, it's shut today. Just a minute, I'll let you in.'

'No, thank you. I only want to see the yew tree.'

He climbed down anyway. He was about the same age as Uncle Derek, but smaller and thinner. He was wearing round, metal-rimmed glasses that were mended with sticky tape. His hair was standing on end, and there was a smear of green lichen on his cheek.

'Aren't you one of our new neighbours, at the old Dower House? How are you getting on? Are you having a good time?'

'Yes, thank you,' said Elinor politely, wondering why he called the Madisons 'neighbours'. They were only here for a fortnight, which was nearly over.

'Good, good. I feel responsible, you see, being the old family's last representative. In a way, that is. Though the estate is nothing to do with me now.'

He looked like a workman, but if he was the 'last representative of the old family' maybe he owned the Dower House. Or perhaps he worked for the agents.

'We broke the card table,' she confessed.

'Did you? Well, never mind. I'm sure it's been broken before. I'll come and try to fix it if you like: at least, I will if you remind me . . .'

'Does some of the furniture come from the big old house?' She was thinking of the amber earrings. She didn't want to give them back, but she was curious about their history – though something told her that she'd be better off not knowing.

The man rubbed at his green cheek with a dirty hand, and shook his head. 'No, not at all. The agents refurnished the place from scratch a couple of years ago. Don't worry, there are no heirlooms at stake.'

'But what about the things in the panelled room? The fourposter bed, and the walnut desk?'

He looked surprised. 'Oh, you mean in the back wing? Yes, now I remember, there were a few pieces from the old house left in there. Sorry, I was talking about the rental part. I thought that wing was shut up.'

'We found the key. I'm sleeping in there.' Elinor blushed, afraid she was stumbling into trouble, revealing that the Madisons had invaded forbidden territory. 'In the room with the fourposter bed. I hope that's all right. Auntie Sylvia didn't want to use the sofa-bed in the study because –'

But he seemed eager to wave her explanations away. 'It's all right. It isn't my business, but I'm sure the agents wouldn't mind. That wing's only kept locked because it hasn't been modernised. How did you know the desk was walnut? Did somebody tell you?'

'I just knew. I like old-fashioned things.'

'I can see that you might. You have an old-fashioned face. Don't be offended, I mean it as a compliment. What's your name, by the way?'

'Elinor.'

'Nice name. Well, Elinor, you must ask your mother if you can come to tea at the Rectory. I'm David Vernon, by the way, I'm the vicar here. In fact, why don't you all come today? I should have invited you before but it slipped my mind. I'm so terribly absent-minded, it's shocking. Look, why don't you come in now and meet Mrs Manaton, my housekeeper? We could phone about tea, and I could show you a few more old-fashioned things.'

He had apparently forgotten about the gutter. She noticed that he'd left the tools he'd been using perched on the roof. 'I have to go,' she said. She didn't have the courage to explain that she was only a cousin. The vicar was nice, and he meant well. But she would rather have had a moment under her yew tree. 'They're waiting for the bread. I'll tell them.'

Aunt Sylvia was overjoyed, though annoyed that the invitation had come through Elinor. None of the Madisons ever went to church, but tea at the Rectory was just the sort of rural socialising Auntie Sylvia dreamed about. She called the Rectory at once and accepted, in her most gushing voice. Elinor wondered why it was such a big deal. But as she gathered the things the family would need for the day (camcorder, story tapes, personal stereos, guidebook, maps, picnic, sun-cream, drinks, bag of snackfood . . .) she was thinking about the amber earrings. Soon the holiday would be over. Would she really dare to steal them? Where could she keep them at home? Nathalie and Megan regularly went through her belongings, making sure she didn't have anything they wanted: and so did Auntie Sylvia, making sure she had no secrets. She'd have to leave them behind. But she was glad she hadn't told the nice vicar about them. The jewels would be hers forever in a way, because no one else knew that they existed.

The morning was spent moving as rapidly as possible, in convoy with all the other tourists, from moorland sight to sight. They visited an ancient cist grave, a standing stone, a famous group of rocks called Hound Tor, and a clapper bridge. The day grew hotter and hotter. By lunchtime, relations inside the Espace had hit a spectacular low. Nathalie and Megan were furious because they'd wanted a last day on the beach; their mother wounded because her children were so hostile, and Uncle Derek was in a silent sulk. Auntie Sylvia decided to give up. They would not picnic and explore on the moor this afternoon. They would have lunch at the pub in Widecombe, and then Nathalie, Megan and Elinor, since they were so sick of sightseeing, could cycle back to the Dower House on their own. Auntie Sylvia, Uncle Derek and little Derek would complete the sightseeing programme in peace, and everyone would regroup at the house in time to drive to the Rectory.

This plan was set into action, in bitterness and recrimination. The three girls trudged up the hill out of Widecombe, which was too steep even for Nathalie and Megan's splendid new mountain bikes. 'It's *your* fault,' said Nathalie. 'You smell, you dirty little servant girl. You don't wash. *That's* why we have to cycle back. Mum couldn't stand having you in the car, and she couldn't send you off by yourself or you'd go whining to the vicar or someone.'

'I didn't –' began Elinor. But it was useless to argue.

'Saying we mistreat you or something. Creep. We should take your bike and junk it, shove it under a speeding car. We should make you walk all the way.'

They'd reached the top of the hill. As there weren't any speeding cars in sight, Nathalie gave up this idea for the moment, jumped on to her bike and sped away. Megan followed, turning round once to stick out her tongue.

Dartmoor in August is not an ideal place for cycling. The hills are many, the lanes are narrow and tourist cars are frequent, on the most minor roads. Elinor, whose second-hand bike had no working gears at all, didn't care how many times she had to get off and walk. She wasn't anxious to catch up. There were brambles and wild strawberries in the banks, and butterflies fluttered over the late summer flowers. Sometimes she passed a field of peaceful cows, sometimes she reached a vantage point from which she could see the whole sweep of the moor rising above the fields. It had not been much fun, but she felt almost sorry that the holiday was over. Finally she reached a lonely hilltop crossroads, moorland behind her and narrow wooded valleys below. She wondered what had happened to the sisters. The deadly morning hours she'd spent in the back of the Espace: sweaty, carsick and continually tortured, had restored her dream of revenge. Maybe the charm would work today. Maybe she would come across Nathalie and Megan somewhere ahead, spread across the road in a mess of mashed flesh and twisted metal.

Meantime, in the real world, she'd better try to catch up. If the trip to the Rectory was delayed because of Elinor there'd be trouble. Nathalie had the map, but Elinor knew she wasn't far from the house now. One of the arms on the crossroads post – which had a name of its own, Dartmoor style: it was called 'Black Hill' – directed her to 'Revelle House'. It didn't mention the Dower House, but she knew the little lane that plunged downward between the trees ought to join the farm track that ran between the derelict big house and their holiday home. She was still wondering what had become of Nathalie and Megan. Suppose something had actually happened to them, because of the pact she'd made with evil for a pair of amber earrings? She felt a moment's tingling fear, a mixture of dread and excitement. Then suddenly, two figures leapt out in front of her, yelling.

Elinor shouted, she swerved. Her bike careered over a bump in the lane, and flew on down the violently steep slope beyond. Both her feet had left the pedals, she had completely lost control. A crossing track rushed towards her. A farm jeep was coming down it, the cab bobbing above the hedgetops. Her bike hit a stone and bucked like a bronco, flinging her over the front wheel, right into its path.

She lay with her cheek smashed against gravel, not sure what was happening except that she didn't think she could move. She had no memory of hitting the ground. But here she was. She could see the thick tyre of a jeep, and she heard a man's voice with a West Country burr.

'Are you all right, my dear?'

'She wasn't looking! It was her own fault!'

That was Nathalie. Nathalie's voice.

'I saw her,' chimed in Megan, self-righteously. 'She didn't even try to stop.'

'Yeah,' came the man's voice again, indignant and stern. 'And *I* saw what you two did, you stupid young devils. What are you, here on holiday? Where are you staying?'

Elinor wondered where Nathalie and Megan had sprung from, and her dizzy memory provided the picture. Her cousins jumping out of the hedge, waving their arms as Elinor came down the hill. They had been lying in ambush.

'It was my spell,' she whispered. 'Harm came to me, instead . . .'

'Never mind your spill,' said the farmer. 'It wasn't your fault. Tell me where it hurts.'

'Don't tell,' she begged, trying to sit up. '*Please don't tell!* Don't tell tales!'

He put the three bikes in the back of his jeep (Elinor's was in a sorry state) and helped Elinor into the cab, after he'd checked that she had no broken bones. He made Nathalie and Megan walk behind as he drove slowly to the Dower House. He meant well. He didn't know that he was making things worse for Elinor, when he told Auntie Sylvia exactly what Megan and Nathalie had done.

She was put to bed in the fourposter room. She felt feverish and strange and her head ached horribly, but she didn't want to go to bed. It was broad daylight. The kindly farmer had told Auntie Sylvia that Elinor ought to be taken to hospital; or at least they ought to call a doctor. She had been knocked out, if only briefly. They ought to make sure she didn't have concussion. Elinor knew they wouldn't, it would be far too much trouble. They were late for the Rectory tea. But she didn't mind not going to the doctor, so long as she didn't have to stay alone in this room.

'Please don't leave me alone!' she begged. 'I hate this room, the bed gives me bad dreams, please don't leave me –' She had never before said a word about her nightmares, or the fourposter bed's hateful power. She'd been proud of that silence, proud of the way she'd kept up her resolve to fight back in her own quiet way. Maybe, all the while, she'd believed that if she finally broke down her aunt would listen, and let her sleep somewhere else. No one would deliberately make a child sleep in a room that terrified her: not even if the child was only a poor relation . . .

But her aunt was angry. The farmer had been disgusted at the dangerous trick Nathalie and Megan had played. He'd spoken his mind. He'd as good as said they were delinquents and implied that Auntie Sylvia wasn't fit to be a mother. Of course it was Elinor's fault. Elinor felt the blame in her aunt's hands, as she applied brusque first-aid.

'Don't be ridiculous. You've too much imagination, that's your problem. And I'm not going to encourage it. Now go to sleep.'

'Let me lie on the sofa in the front room. Please, don't leave me alone in here –'

'Go to sleep,' said her aunt stonily. She had taken the evil, rock-heavy eiderdown out of the blanket chest. She dumped it over her niece like someone burying a piece of rubbish. She closed the curtains at Elinor's window, shutting out the light and air, and left without a backward glance.

The dream, when it came, was different from anything that had happened to her in the fourposter room before; and yet strangely familiar. Hard, angry hands shook her shoulders. She opened her eyes and found herself staring – too close – into her aunt's painted face: white powdered cheeks, red mouth and dark arched brows.

'Get up, you lazy slut! Get up and to your work, ungrateful creature –'

She was not in the panelled room. She was in another, much bigger place: and the light was different. It came shining in through a row of deep-set mullioned windows. Her bed was a crackling straw-pallet on a low wooden frame. On the other side of the room there was another bed, much grander but not a fourposter. A little boy lay in it, sleeping. Her aunt was gone, in a swirl of coloured skirts. She must be up and to her chores. She dressed and went outside to wash herself in ice-cold water at the pump in the kitchen yard. It was long past dawn. She had over-slept herself, no wonder Aunt was angry. It was winter-time. First she must mend the fire, and fetch water. Then she must wake her charge, wash him, dress him, fetch his breakfast.

She carried a slopping bucket across the yard, a bundle of kindling under her other arm, her wooden pattens cracking the frozen mud. One of the maids came to the kitchen door and laughed at her. 'Oh, Nelly, thou art a slugabed. The pigs shall have your porridge, my lass, and you shall have a whipping!'

Suddenly, everything came back to her. She was not 'Elinor'. No one had called her by her pretty Christened name since mother died. She was Nelly. Her mother and her father and her brothers and sisters were all dead. Her aunt had sent for her from London to be nursemaid to her husband's child: the little boy called Diccon. The lovely, angry lady who had woken her just now was her Aunt Deborah, who was a famous beauty, and had married a gentleman.

It was hard work to be a nursemaid. She slept in the

same room as Diccon. She fetched his meals, dressed him, washed him, played with him: emptied out the slops from his chamberpot and washed the pot afterwards. She did all his laundry and ironing, sometimes cooked for him; kept everything in their rooms clean and shining. But it was not a bad life, except for the real servants of the great house. They had quickly learned that their mistress's poor relation need not be treated gently. Nelly tried to keep out of their way, because the maids would order her to help with their own tasks if they got the chance, and she didn't dare to complain. She had to satisfy everyone or she'd get her ears boxed and no supper.

Diccon was her comfort. In some ways he was a baby. He was six years old but he would sit and wait for her to dress him, amazed if she delayed or expected him to lift a hand. In other ways he was old and wise beyond his years. Rarely, he'd get on his dignity in the middle of a game and declare he could not play with Nelly because he was a gentleman's son. Nearly always, they played together tenderly. He could read and write and even knew a little Latin – taught by the pious and learned lady, his dead mother. He would try to teach Nelly her letters; or read to her solemnly from one of his prayer books. When she cried in the night for her mother, her father and her brothers and sisters, all swept away by a cruel fever, the sad little boy would come to her and kiss her, and tell Nelly that their mothers were happy together in heaven.

Diccon's father was a distant figure. He didn't often call the child to his presence. The servants said he didn't want to be reminded of his dead lady. This was another sadness, added to the loss of his mother, that the child bore in patient silence. Aunt Deborah was very different. She was, to both the children (for Nelly was only a child herself) something like a fierce goddess. Her slaps and cuffs were freely bestowed on Nelly. Though she never touched her husband's child, Diccon was afraid of her. But she was lovely, and she fascinated them. When Aunt Deborah was away in London they had a more peaceful life, but they missed the excitement.

Nelly strained her childish muscles at the hard domestic tasks, and gazed as if from a vast distance at the beautiful possessions her aunt, her own mother's sister, had won by her brilliant marriage: the gowns, the fine lace, the jewels; the grand halls of this great house, the splendid horses and carriages. She felt no resentment. She even understood that Aunt Deborah took satisfaction in keeping her poor niece as a servant. When she slapped and chided Nelly, she was triumphing over her own humble past. But there was something wrong. Elinor, who looked out of Nelly's eyes, knew that there was something *wrong*: something that nagged at her through the enchantment of this incredibly real dream. A hidden menace.

Aunt Deborah had sent for Diccon. She was entertaining several ladies in the south drawing room, hung in new sea-green, that overlooked a pleasant view of the home meadows and the village church. Nelly brought him to the door, inspected him one last time for cleanliness and neatness and then waited outside. She heard the delicate voices, chattering like birds. Aunt Deborah was announcing her plans for the old house and grounds. She would have fountains in the gardens. The village church that spoiled her 'vista' would be demolished. She had drawings, done for her by a master draughtsman, showing the 'Grecian temple' that would stand in its place. The West Country ladies were shocked and admiring. Like Nelly, they found the new mistress of Revelle House a fascinating spectacle.

A bell chimed, and she knew she was to take Diccon away.

She barely saw the room or its contents: she was too shy to look at the ladies. She was concentrating on getting Diccon away without either of them annoying Aunt Deborah.

A voice said, 'But still no family expectations, my dear?' She heard her aunt's tinkling laugh. 'Please, none of your country indelicacies! My niece and her charge are over young for such subjects!' Diccon came to her side out of a blur of coloured gowns and polished furniture. He clutched her hand.

'She is a good girl,' said Aunt Deborah. 'It was an excellent thought of mine to bring her here for the child, so that I may devote myself to my husband's career. The social round in London is so tedious, but I will endure anything to further our family's interests.'

For a moment the ladies were strangely silent. Nelly hung her head, guessing what a poor figure she must make, though she'd combed her hair and her cap was clean.

'Don't stand like a mommet, Nelly. Take the child away!'

She bobbed a courtesy. As they turned to leave, Aunt Deborah flew from her chair in a rush of canary silk petticoats, fell on the little boy and kissed him passionately. Her amber ear drops, which she always wore with that yellow gown, glowed against the child's soft skin.

'I dote on him!' she cried. 'My husband's child, if God wish it, shall be my only dear!'

In an undertone, giving Elinor a shrewd pinch on the arm, she hissed, 'I had to ring twice, slut. Be off with you.'

As Nelly and Diccon crossed the oak-beamed entrance hall, dark and bare and cavernous in the manner of an older day, she felt disturbed by currents of danger that she didn't understand. The little boy looked up into her face, eyes full of fear and puzzled woe. Why was he so afraid?

Time passed. On another day, Nelly carried a crisp armful of lace-trimmed garments to her aunt's bed chamber. She had been living with the Revelles for a long time, by her childish reckoning. She was so deft and careful with her smoothing irons that she had been given charge of all the household's fine linen. The house was in great excitement, because Mistress Deborah was at last with child. Her husband was pleased. (More pleased than he had been when he rejected her elegant plans to demolish the ancient church). He was hoping for a daughter. So was his wife, or so she said. Nelly felt sorry for the bold lady, who would be tamed by motherhood: no longer riding her horses; no longer making those great journeys to join the fashionable world in London. But Aunt Deborah had spoken of sending Diccon away to school. What would become of his nursemaid then?

Her heart trembled. What would become of Diccon, without his Nelly?

The room was empty. She glanced at the handsome walnut desk, made for Diccon's mother, a piece of furniture for which Mistress Deborah, no great writer, had little use; and set her burden on a side table for Mistress Deborah's maid to put away. Her own hand, red and rough and swollen about the nails, lay against the folds of delicate white lawn. She imagined with fierce hunger how it might feel to wear something so smooth and fine.

He is a gentleman's son, she thought. *Why should I pity him?*

Then, fearfully, she approached her aunt's dressing table. There, in a litter of unguent jars, paints and powders, lay the yellow ear-bobs. They were not the most costly of her aunt's jewels but Nelly loved them the best. There was something curiously magical and forbidden about those glowing drops, with the tiny flies caught inside. If you rubbed a paper or a piece of silk against them it would cling to the smooth surface, like a living thing trapped and helpless. She heard sharp, light footsteps and turned with a guilty start, the ear-bobs clutched in her hand. There stood her aunt, with the strangest expression on her bold, lovely face . . .

At that moment, Elinor suddenly knew again that she was dreaming. She seemed to fall, as if she'd been jerked forcibly out of Nelly's body. But the yellow ear-bobs were still in her hand. *I wanted them!* she heard herself crying. The voice did not sound like hers. It spoke with a thick accent, the words hardly sounded like English. But she knew it was her own.

I wanted the yellow ear-bobs!

'Wake up! Wake up, Elinor.'

She struggled back to consciousness. The aches and pains that had been natural to the other Elinor became the cuts and bruises from her bike fall. She had been away such a long time. She felt that she had lived for years in that other world: she was bewildered to find that the bruises were still hurting.

'I've had such a dream –'

She was back in the fourposter room. Already her dream was unravelling. Scenes that had been clear and distinct fell into fragments. Auntie Sylvia was frowning at her impatiently.

'We had a lovely tea, thank you very much for asking. But it's late, it's nearly eight o'clock. You'd better get up, it's time to put Dekkie to bed.'

'Yes'm. At once, mistress.' She tried to stand. She must fetch the hot water. But where was Diccon? He must be somewhere close by, she could hear him crying. The room swayed. 'My head aches,' she complained timidly. 'There's a funny noise in my ears.' She sat down again without meaning to. She couldn't stop trembling. 'My eyes feel so hot.'

Elinor had a touch of the sun, and her various bruises had swollen and stiffened alarmingly. Even Auntie Sylvia had to admit she wasn't fit to get up. She was sent to have a warm bath and put back to bed with two paracetamol; and for once she slept without dreams.

For two days she was left alone. Auntie Sylvia appeared at long intervals, bringing drinks and meals. In between, Elinor lay for hours slipping in and out of a troubled doze. She dreamed that she was asleep beside the hollow yew in the churchyard, and that she was woken by the sound of a child crying: a sound that filled her with inexplicable dread. She dreamed that she was walking along a stony track. Grey hills loomed in the distance on either side, there was one stark tree. She had never seen this place before, but as she walked she became more and more afraid, until she was ready to scream . . . Sometimes she woke from one of these puzzling dreams with a horrible conviction that *she had done something terrible.* But she could not remember what it was. She would lie in dull despair, feeling that evil had her in its power. She would live and die like this, sunk in hateful visions, trapped by the stifling bedcurtains, the panelled walls closing around her . . . Until Auntie Sylvia came marching in with a tray, and the spell was broken.

On the last evening she was well enough to get up. The bustle of cleaning and tidying the Dower House released her from the grip of those trance-like nightmares. Next morning she climbed into the back of the car with the others, her normal self again and bracing herself for the trials of the journey. As the Espace climbed the narrow lane for the last time she remembered the amber and silver earrings. They were still tucked under the mattress of the fourposter bed. She had forgotten to return them to their original hiding place. It was a horrible shock. She had meant to return them! She wasn't a thief! She was so frightened that she almost begged Uncle Derek to turn back. Of course she didn't dare to make such a crazy request. But the feeling of panic persisted. She told herself she'd done nothing wrong, she'd only scribbled a few silly words on a piece of paper: she hadn't even taken the earrings out of that room. And anyway she was never coming back here. There was no reason to be afraid.

It was no use. She could feel the Dower House behind her, even when that narrow valley was miles and miles away. It was still watching, with the cold and thankless eyes of its windows. She knew that it would not forget.

Part Two

Four

THE REST OF THE SUMMER HOLIDAYS PASSED normally. There were trips to the cinema, trips to the beach, shopping expeditions, meals out. Elinor endured the life of a poor relation: everyone's scapegoat when things went wrong, happiest when she was left at home alone. Nathalie gave up the '*pwactically before I was born*' chant, and invented a rhyme about Elinor's stick-insect legs. The only unusual feature of these weeks was that Auntie Sylvia was very busy, so there was more babysitting than usual. This was fine by Elinor. The young woman who came to look after Dekkie and keep an eye on the girls (this part was greatly resented by Nathalie), didn't know the rules of the Madison household. She treated Nathalie, Elinor and Megan as if they were equals, and even seemed to *prefer* Elinor. Elinor decided Auntie Sylvia must be trying to get a job. This was something she'd often threatened, since Dekkie started school.

When term began Elinor knew that something inside her had changed, since the holiday in the Dower House. She had not had a good time. The fourposter room and its nightmares would haunt her for years. But, strangely, when she looked back on those two weeks what she remembered best was her meeting with Mr Vernon the vicar. (She supposed she should call him Reverend Vernon, but it sounded too peculiar). It had been a very brief, ordinary conversation: but that was the point. He had treated her like an ordinary, interesting person. Not the despised outsider but Elinor, with the 'old-fashioned face', who knew about furniture and liked old-fashioned things. For a few moments she had *felt* like that person. It made her think.

She wasn't going to cry herself to sleep any more, wondering why her aunt hated her and her cousins bullied her. She would stop seeing herself through the Madisons' eyes. She would become *herself*: someone who would one day be old enough to leave the Madisons behind, and have a life of her own.

On one of the first days of term she noticed the boy called Ryan, who'd asked her about her burns. He was smiling as they passed on the stairs. Of course this brought back the old Elinor. She cringed, convinced he was laughing at her. But the new Elinor, the one who was fighting back, managed to return the smile.

I don't care, she thought. If he despises me because I thought my mother was dead when she's only run off with someone, then too bad for him.

A few days later they accidentally met outside school. Ryan was waiting for the bus. Elinor was waiting for the mother who was doing the school run that week. Auntie Sylvia and several other mothers had a regular rota for picking up their children. Nathalie was talking loudly with a group of her friends, Elinor standing uneasily beside them.

'Hi,' said Ryan.

'Hello,' responded Elinor doubtfully. The flowerbeds at the school gates were planted with roses surrounded by borders of lavender. They were battered by short-cut takers, but some of the scent and colour survived. She picked a sprig of dusty violet and rubbed it between her fingers. Ryan, with another shy smile, did the same.

'I've been wanting to talk to you,' he began. 'About that

time before the end of term, when I asked you how you got burned. I'm sorry if that was rude. I didn't mean it to come out the way it did . . . Hey, this smells good. What's it called?'

'Lavender.'

'Mmm. I'll remember.' He shook his head, grinning. 'Only I don't think it would grow in Asabaland. Too much heat and too much rain.'

'It's all right,' said Elinor. 'I don't know why I said what I did, about my mother. I really knew she was gone, not dead. But it was all so long ago. If people don't talk to you about what happened when you were a little child you have to make up your own stories, and things get confused. People don't talk to children enough, do they, about important things. They mean well, I suppose.'

Ryan nodded bitterly. 'Yeah. I suppose they mean well.'

That gave her a surprise. He sounded as if he knew exactly, miserably, what she was talking about. 'Is that where you come from?'

'Where?'

'Asabaland. It's in Africa, isn't it?'

'Yeah. It's next to Nigeria. It's a pretty nice place. It didn't use to be, it used to be horrible, but we had a revolution a few years ago . . . Maybe you heard about that?'

Elinor shook her head. She didn't know a thing about world politics. 'D'you get homesick?'

'You bet.' Ryan looked at her sidelong, as if he was testing something out. 'I cry myself to sleep, sometimes,' he announced, very casually.

Elinor, before she could stop herself, nodded. 'Me too.'

'My parents sent me over here to get a UK education,' he went on, in a firmer voice. 'My dad says it's still the best in the world. They pay for me to stay with some people, a "host family" out in the lovely . . . English . . . countryside.' He spoke these last three words very bitterly, through gritted teeth.

'Don't you like it?'

Ryan's eyes flashed. Then he shrugged. 'I suppose it's okay. I suppose they mean well. But my name's not Ryan,' he added, like someone hesitating on the brink, and then taking a plunge. 'It's Oyadipo. *She* calls me "Ryan", because *she* says Oyadipo is too hard to pronounce.'

Elinor instantly knew who *she* was. She didn't have to know this person's name. She recognised another 'Aunt Sylvia'. Someone who wasn't your mother and did not care.

'What a cheek.'

He shrugged again, resignedly. 'Can't do anything about it. My parents don't know. I mean, they're paying a lot of money and it's important to them. What can I say?'

'You should tell them.'

'Yeah. Suppose I should.'

They were both silent, rubbing the lavender and inhaling the soothing, astringent balm of its perfume. There was no need for Ryan to explain that he would never tell. Elinor knew. She could have been offended, because this odd boy had obviously picked her out as another outsider, another loser in the game of life. But she was not. She admired his nerve.

'You could call me Oya,' he suggested.

'Yes, I could. I will.' She grinned at him. 'You could call me Lin. My name's Elinor, but Lin is what my dad used to call me. When I grow up –' (She had just decided this, but it sounded right and good), 'I'm going to call myself Lin O'Falloren.'

'That's an unusual name.'

'It was my mother's. That's my mother's name. I don't have to be called Madison. When I'm old enough, I'll change it by deed poll. That's what you have to do. I read about it.'

A horn tooted. Nathalie shrieked. 'Elinor! Elinor, stop messing about –'

'Got to go. See you tomorrow. Good luck with – with the "*English countryside.*"'

If it had been up to Elinor, it would have been weeks before she plucked up the courage to speak to Oya again. In spite of her good resolutions she found it hard to believe that anyone actually wanted to make friends with her. As long as she'd been in this school, and at Primary School before that, Nathalie's friends were the only 'friends' Elinor had ever had: always the biggest girls, the smartly-dressed ones, the ones who had the fanciest possessions. Her life had been spent trailing round after Nathalie's clique, being teased and despised. That was what seemed natural. But Oya didn't wait for Elinor to make the running. He came looking for her at break and lunchtimes. He said hello and stopped to chat whenever their paths crossed. He generally had an excuse: photos of his family and their house in Gerardville in Africa; a book he thought she'd like to read; a question about some school work. But it was obvious that he was taking Elinor under his wing. Gradually, she began to trust him. He told her about the trials of life with his 'host family': the uncaring silence of that house, where only the TV was allowed to talk; the horrible food they made him eat. She told him about the Madisons. Their plight was the same. They could be allies.

Nathalie, to Elinor's surprise, didn't seem able to prevent what was happening. When Oya came along and said, 'Hi, Lin. Got something I want to show you', Elinor could *walk away* from the group: and no one could stop her. She was astonished. She began to suspect, several years late, that she had always been free. She had been caught in the prison of her own misery.

Then, just as she had begun to relax, something terrible happened.

Auntie Sylvia had been talking about moving to the country since Derek had grown too big for his cot. She wanted to live graciously. She wanted him to have the advantages of a small, rural primary school; she wanted Megan and Nathalie to have ponies and know the right sort of people. Elinor was used to hearing this project discussed. On the Dower House holiday she'd trailed around a few plush, swanky gardens with Dekkie, while Nathalie and Megan and their parents inspected a house. But the hunt hadn't seemed serious. Maybe if she'd asked she'd have been told what was happening. She had not thought of asking. She didn't expect to be included in the discussion of Madison family plans.

It was on a Wednesday morning that the bomb dropped. It was breakfast time. Auntie Sylvia was talking with Uncle Derek in the dining room. He usually scooted straight out to the office as soon as he'd eaten, so Elinor knew something was up. The children were in the kitchen. Megan and Dekkie were eating cereal at the breakfast bar. Nathalie was drinking a glass of water with lemon juice, and eating half a grilled grapefruit without sugar. Elinor was packing Dekkie's lunch. Auntie Sylvia came in. Her face was rather pink and her eyes bright. 'Children, I have something to tell you.'

Nathalie picked up a grapefruit segment and studied it carefully, searching for hidden deposits of fat. Derek, for no apparent reason, reached out and smacked Megan on the back of her hand with his milky cereal spoon.

'*Mum!*' squealed Megan. 'Stop him!'

'Stop that, Dekkie darling. Well, everything's settled.

We have exchanged contracts. We're moving into the Dower House at half-term. Isn't that wonderful!'

Nathalie instantly flew into a rage. '*Half-term!* You can't do that! I have things to do at half-term. You can't disrupt everything and make me spend my time *packing*!'

'But darling, you said you wanted to move. You know you have friends at school who live near Breadford. There's Caroline Ransome, and Freda Thorne. You remember, Freda's mother's going to help us buy you a pony –'

'I want to move, okay, if you insist, but I didn't know it was going to be *this half-term*. You've got no consideration, you never asked me. Why can't *you* do the move, in schooltime, instead of sitting on your fat behind all day watching TV?'

Elinor stared at the sandwich bread, dumbfounded. The Dower House? *It couldn't be.* It must be some other 'Dower House', or she must have misheard . . .

Auntie Sylvia's happiness was for once impervious to her daughter's rude remarks.

'Don't worry. The removal people will do everything, and Elinor will help you to pack –'

'*She's not going to touch anything of mine!*'

Derek started yelling furiously, 'NOT DEKKIE! Call me Derek, stupid Mummy!'

Megan whined loudly. 'Mum, I'm going to have a pony too, aren't I? Mum, Mum, I am going to have a pony, and Elinor isn't getting one –'

It can't be true, thought Elinor desperately. *It can't be.* Uncle Derek will save me. He hates the idea of moving. Her uncle put his head round the door. 'I'm off to work,' he informed the throbbing room. 'I see you've told them the big news, then. Great pub, the Flying Fish.'

It was true. They had not thought of buying the Dower

House when they rented it, though they knew the property was for sale. But they had looked at other places, and there was none so convenient, so near the motorway, so close to a good school for Derek in Eaxby; and with Nathalie's two best (meaning smartest and richest) friends living nearby. And one can't go on house-hunting forever. Auntie Sylvia had come to love the idea of *doing up* the Dower House: fitting out those shut-up rooms, landscaping the garden. They could live in the rental part while the work was being done so Auntie Sylvia would be able to supervise the workmen. The whole thing was perfect.

Elinor soon picked up the facts, once she knew what the Madisons were talking about. She felt numb. It was just her luck to have to move, when she'd made a friend of her own for the first time since Dad died. She'd probably have to change schools, and go to somewhere 'select' in the country, with Megan and Nathalie. But why did it have to be that house? She remembered the place with dread. She couldn't believe she would have to live there.

That evening, in a small, shabby house on the edge of the village of Breadford, Oya was completing his evening chores. Mrs McDonald and her husband were watching television, their sixteen-year-old son Joe was in his room playing extremely loud music. Oya did the washing up, mopped the floor and finally let the two alsations, Grip and Trigger back into the kitchen to be fed. This was a job he hated. He was afraid of the big dogs, and they knew it. He hated the smell of them – which seemed to get all over the house, mingled with the smell of long-boiled vegetables. Sometimes they fouled the kitchen. Oya had to clean it up, no one else would.

He cut up a disgusting grey and red mess called 'lights', while the brutes snarled and glowered. Once when he was a little boy he had been given a puppy, by some German tourists. They had bought it from the pygmy hunters they'd met on a forest trek, and then couldn't take it home with them. His grandma had refused to let him keep it. 'Not in the house!' she'd roared. 'Not in the house! A hunting dog is not a pet!' Oya had cried and cried, but his dad and mum agreed with Grandma and the puppy had to go. How Oya had *hated* the old lady: and how he wished his grandma was here now, to roar at the MacDonalds '*Not in the house!*' and drive Grip and Trigger out into the MacDonalds' unclean back yard. Grandma never stood any nonsense from anyone.

At last it was done. He left the dogs snapping at each other and wolfing their food, and retired upstairs, sneaking on tiptoe past the open door of the front room, where only the TV ever spoke. His bedroom was chilly. *She* wouldn't let him have the central heating on. *She* had no conception of a climate different from her own. She didn't believe he could be cold in September. He dreaded another English winter. But it would be better than last year. He was more used to things now. He put on an extra sweater, took off his shoes and got into bed in his clothes. He'd discovered that if he did this he would have made himself a cave of warmth by the time he wanted to go to sleep, when he could quickly dive along to the bathroom, wash, and get back to bed in his pyjamas before the warmth had faded. He'd supplied himself with writing things, a chunk of cheese and some pitta bread in a sandwich box, a bottle of drinking water and, lastly, a box of pink wax earplugs he had bought from the chemists.

Now he was ready for anything. He imagined that he was in his bunk on a big old sailing ship, the way his great grandfather had once travelled to Paris. It must have been chilly on that journey, too. The end of this cold voyage would be the end of his English schooling, when he would return home in triumph, having endured all hardships.

He put the earplugs into his ears. The harsh beat of Joe's music became a distant thunder: the ocean waves were pounding at his ship's timbers.

He began to write, in black ink, forming the letters in a beautiful clear, curving style.

Dear Mummy and Daddy. I have made a new friend

Maybe he should say, 'I hope I have made a friend,' in case his claim turned out to be an idle boast. But he decided to trust Lin, and be glad for what he had. (That was another thing Grandma used to say.)

Her name is Lin O'Falloren, but at the moment she's living with her father's relatives, who are called Madison.

He paused again. The name O'Falloren was familiar to him, and he'd wondered briefly if Lin could be any connection with his parents' good friend. But Lin didn't know anything about Africa, so it seemed unlikely. For all he knew, O'Falloren was a common name in Britain; and only sounded unusual to a foreigner.

She's in my year but not in my class. I've heard people say she is clever. She reads a lot. She has long hair, which she sometimes wears in a pony tail and sometimes in two braids wound around her head. Both ways are rather nice-looking.

Thanks for the money. I'm going to spend most of it on really good swimming goggles. In swimming I have learned to do racing turns. In Maths we are doing mystic rose patterns. It's very fascinating. Maths and swimming are my best subjects. And history, too. That's all for now. I'm working hard and looking forward VERY

much to Christmas. Love to the kids, and my respect and love to Grandma. Tell my sister Opie that I'm training up my hair-pulling muscles just for her benefit.
Love XXXXXX from Oya.

Five

THEY MOVED IN ON OCTOBER 29TH. THE weather was cool, still and misty. Uncle Derek had planned to take the day off work, but had found out at the last minute that he couldn't make it. He'd promised to be with them later in the afternoon. Auntie Sylvia, with Megan, Dekkie and Elinor, arrived just ahead of the removal van. Nathalie had been dropped off at her friend Freda's house. Freda's parents ran a riding school. Nathalie was going to have a ride, with Freda and their friend Caroline, and discuss what kind of pony she should buy.

Elinor had been so happy to discover that she wouldn't have to change schools and that Oya actually lived in Breadford, she'd decided she could cope with living in the Dower House. She would never be able to return the earrings to their proper hiding place now, because obviously all the old furniture would be gone. But she had managed to put that silly, nagging idea about the curse out of her mind. If things had been different, she'd have loved to come and live in the country: well, she would *make* things different. She was disappointed when she stood again on that gravel parking-space, looked at the house and felt the same instant dislike as she had felt in the summer. Megan and Derek scrambled out and ran off into the garden.

'Shall I start taking the suitcases in?' asked Elinor,

determined to be positive. Auntie Sylvia had other ideas.

'Off you go, Elinor dear. I don't want you under the men's feet. Go for a walk.'

Elinor was rather stunned at being called 'dear'. But she didn't argue.

The leaves on the trees around the lawn had changed colour, and the vegetable beds looked forlorn. She walked around the garden, wondering why the Madisons didn't feel the same way as she did. She thought she must be like a dog or a cat, whining and disturbed by one of those whistles that makes a sound beyond the range of human hearing. The removal van had begun to manoeuvre through the gateway. She could see that it was going to crunch into one of the posts. Auntie Sylvia had hurried out of the house and was gesturing madly, pointing the driver in exactly the wrong direction. Elinor thought of trying to help, but she knew she'd only end up in trouble. She slipped through the thin patch in the trees, an unofficial exit that Megan and Dekkie had found in the summer, and escaped.

Beyond the house the grass-grown asphalt soon degenerated into a stony track. She had never been this way in the summer, except that time when she was brought back in the farmer's jeep. She reached a bridge where the stream that had followed the lane ran under it, and sat there, perched on the mossy parapet, listening to the water. A bunch of hornbeam keys came twirling down from over her head. She caught them in her lap. Every falling leaf you catch in autumn means you'll have one happy day in the next year. She wondered what catching a bunch of keys might mean. She didn't expect to be happy, not for a long while. But a key is a seedcase. Maybe this move to Breadford held seeds of happiness.

She had spent the last evening, after the final packing was done, kneeling on her bed in the Madisons' house in town: silently saying goodbye to her friends and neighbours in the dark street below. They lived in a quiet backstreet of tall old houses built from thin red bricks; most of them divided into flats. There were always people passing. There was the nice-looking red haired woman at number 33, whose three tabby cats waited for her on the steps outside her house, and ran, mewing, to greet her as she came home from work. The man who played the violin so beautifully in an upstairs lamplit room behind white net curtains. The three girl students who had a flat at number 40, who marched along in a row whenever they were together, blocking the pavement and talking noisily. They always looked so happy. The people who put up a brightly-lit Christmas tree by mid-November, without fail. The people who had a whole bedroom full of huge houseplants, like a jungle. She'd barely spoken to any of them. But she had felt that she belonged to the street, in a secret way: it sort of made up for the fact that she would never belong to the Madison family.

Elinor's room had been on the third floor, next to Derek's domain – a much bigger room with space for all his toys. She had not been very fond of it, because it never felt like hers. She'd had to have the same wallpaper and paint as Nathalie, to save trouble. Maybe, since the whole of the Dower House was going to be redecorated, she'd get a chance to choose her own scheme this time, as long as she didn't ask for anything difficult. She knew what she wanted. The walls should be plain white, because that would show off her pictures best, her Arthur Rackam print that she'd bought from a jumble sale; and the little Victorian engraving that someone had given to Auntie Sylvia and no one else in the house wanted. The woodwork should be a warm yellow. She'd seen the exact colour on one of Auntie Sylvia's paint-shade cards. It was called 'marzipan' for some reason, but was really a lovely clear amber. And then she'd like a new bed, because the pine frame of her old one was broken. She'd like a divan with drawers underneath. And a new desk, and her curtains would have a pattern of oranges and lemons and green leaves . . .

Elinor laughed. 'Fat chance. But I can dream.'

She slipped down from the bridge and walked on. The marshy fields, which had been full of flowers and haunted by vicious horseflies in August, were dull and muddy. Ahead of her the valley opened up and the track wound over its flat bottom like a meandering stream. On either side, moorland rose to the distant horizon. Over on the right she saw the woods that surrounded the big empty house, rising beyond to the Black Hill where she'd fallen off her bike. Away to the left, on the shoulder of the moor, there was a farm. She could see the grey walls of its house and outbuildings. That must be where Mr Davy came from, the farmer who had picked her up in his jeep. It was strange how familiar everything looked. That one jeep ride must have made a big impression, because she seemed to know this track as well as if she'd walked it thousands of times . . .

The mist had cleared, but the air hung wet as dewy cobwebs against her face. It made her feel cold, and fearful. She turned aside at the next field gate and stood leaning on the top bar, trembling. '*What's wrong with me?*' she whispered. It was stupid to be afraid. Living here wouldn't be like the summer. She would be able to go to school on the country bus with Oya. They could explore the moors together – but not until the summer. She knew he hated the cold. She stared into the meadow, trying to distract her mind. A small herd of curly-headed calves stood staring at her, snorting damp dragon-breath. Beyond them she saw the grey hills rising to the sky, the big house among its woods . . .

Elinor gasped. I dreamed this!

Suddenly she knew why the track was familiar. She had walked this path before. Over and over, in her dreams, while her body lay on the hateful fourposter bed, she had trudged here with halting feet, filled with the same mysterious dread that she felt now. She stared into the landscape of her nightmare, remembering that long trance when she had seemed to wake into another world as real as this one. There had been horses and coaches then, in Nelly's time, rumbling along this track. She remembered Aunt Deborah, and Diccon. The clothes she had worn, Diccon's little shirts, Aunt Deborah's wonderful gowns. Getting up in the dark, the smell of tallow candles burning, ice-cold water on her poor chapped hands . . . Her heart began to thump. She knew it was the other Elinor, poor Nelly, who had walked here, step by heavy step, carrying a weight of terror like a sack of lead. But why, why had she been so frightened?

She couldn't remember. She could only remember the fear itself.

Something had disturbed the calves. They started to move towards her gate in a bunch. Elinor returned to the present. She was nervous of big animals. The gate didn't look very sturdy, and in a mass the calves looked huge. She hurriedly backed away.

'Don't worry,' shouted somebody. 'I'm not driving them at you: they just think I am.'

A human being emerged, and pushed fearlessly through the jostling animals. It was a middle-aged lady dressed in a tweed skirt and jacket, green wellingtons and a shapeless fisherman's hat. She was carrying a small open basket. 'Did you want to come through?' she asked, as she heaved up the latch and opened the gate. 'It's very wet underfoot, I warn you.'

'N-no. I was just looking.'

'MOOGH!' groaned the foremost animal. Elinor winced. Slime dripped from its huge wet nostrils. The tweedy lady coolly pushed it aside, and managed to get through the gate without being trampled. She latched it behind her.

'MOOO to you, too,' she said to the calf, and smiled at Elinor. 'They lead such boring lives, poor things. You can't blame them for rushing up like paparazzi. But I'm not visiting them. I was taking a shortcut.' She showed Elinor the contents of her basket. 'A short cut for mushrooms,' she explained, and grinned: showing large, horsy white teeth. 'How d'you do. I'm Sonia Manaton. Aren't you one of the Madison girls, the people who've moved into the Dower House?'

Elinor nodded. 'I'm Elinor. I'm Nathalie and Megan's cousin.'

'Yes, you were the one who didn't come to tea because you'd fallen off your bike.' She peered into her basket. 'Too damp,' she remarked. 'Mist brings out the mushrooms, but one can have too much of a good thing. You'd better have mushrooms on toast for tea today. Within an hour or so, would be best. They're for you people, by the way. Does your mother, I mean your aunt, like field mushrooms?'

'I don't know.'

'Some people are afraid of them. Well, how do you like your new home?'

'I – we've only just arrived.' Elinor remembered that Mrs Manaton was the name of the vicar's housekeeper. 'Did this lane used to be a proper road? Leading to the big house?'

They left the gate. She found herself strolling beside Mrs Manaton, heading back towards the Dower House. She was glad of the company. She hoped it would be all right with Auntie Sylvia. But she'd been gone for ages, she must be expected back by now.

'I don't know about a proper road,' said Mrs Manaton. 'It's never been surfaced beyond the Dower House. Long ago, if that's what you mean, it was the front drive through the park to Revelle House. But there's not much sign of the park left, and the big house has been falling into rack and ruin for a long, long time. It's two hundred years or more since the Revelles were in their heyday. Were you thinking of exploring? For heaven's sake don't go into the big house on your own. It's extremely dangerous.'

'Why is our place called the Dower House?'

'Well, that's another relic, like this track. In the past, as you may know, a married woman kept no property of her own. Any money she brought into the marriage settlement was handed over to her husband: and that's called a dowry. If there was a big house like Revelle Manor she'd be the mistress of it, but only while her husband was alive. After he died her eldest son's wife would become the new first lady. The old first lady might well prefer to move out. That's what a Dower House was for: it would come to her, with an income. A return on the financial investment a fine lady made in her marriage. But the last time *your* house was used like that must have been, oh, when the infamous Deborah Revelle lived there.'

Elinor started: 'Deborah!'

'I see you've heard of her, our wicked lady. She's a famous historical figure, by local standards. We're proud of her.' Mrs Manaton paused and turned to look back. The mist had vanished completely, as it often does towards sunset on cool autumn days. Revelle House, the opposite view to the one Elinor had glimpsed from the churchyard, could be clearly seen.

'When Deborah Revelle first came here there was a very old building on that site, a medieval fortified manor. She was the one who had most of it torn down, the vandal. She rebuilt the place as a grand modern mansion, in the seventeen-eighties or thereabouts. There's a sad story about that. But I don't know if I should tell you, because it concerns your house.'

'I don't mind.'

'Okay then, I will. Deborah was a penniless beauty who married a very rich, very sober Dartmoor gentleman called Simon Revelle. She was ambitious. She wanted a title for her husband and a mansion that would be the envy of the polite world. She came down here very fine and dashing, full of her great plans. It was while the house was being rebuilt that the sad part happened. Deborah moved into the Dower House with her husband's little boy – Richard Revelle, Simon's son by his first wife. She'd sent her husband up to London, probably to keep him from protesting at all the changes. The little boy went out one day on his pony and didn't come home. Must have fallen in a mineshaft, or into one of the sinking bogs. His name is on their tomb in Breadford churchyard, but they never found his body. Simon Revelle never recovered from the loss. He spent years as a recluse and a semi-invalid: became a depressive after the loss of his son, we'd say. Deborah had children of her own, but their father never cared for them by all accounts, and her son ran through a pot of money and left the estate in ruins. She didn't spend a single happy day in her fine new mansion, so the story goes.'

She turned to Elinor, smiling so that the strongly marked laughter lines creased up around her eyes. 'It's not much of a legend, really. I can see you've heard it before. I should have known. You were here in the summer, and I'm sure the Dower House was stuffed with local history leaflets.'

Elinor had been trying to keep her face expressionless.

'Why was she called wicked?'

Sonia laughed. 'To make the history of Breadford

sound more interesting, of course! She shocked the local gentry, with her bold ways. They didn't approve of her because she was an upstart, a foreigner and ambitious. Anyone who comes from east of Eaxby is a foreigner round here. There are tales. She was proud and hard-hearted; and they say she had a smuggler chief for a lover, and used to ride with him in secret and commit dark deeds. It certainly seems that her children treated her cruelly, in the end: which can be a sign that the children have not been loved themselves. But who can tell? I like to give her the benefit of the doubt. If you want wickedness, the smugglers' gang she's supposed to have known about was much better Hallowe'en fare. I could tell you some hair-raising stories about that crew. Some accounts claim that *they* killed the Revelle boy, little Diccon. They kidnapped him for ransom, and something went wrong.'

They had reached the Dower House. The removal van was still there but its open depths were empty. A strange car, a big grey-green Audi, was parked out in the lane beside the crunched gatepost. Auntie Sylvia was in the back porch, chatting to a dark-haired woman Elinor vaguely recognised. It was probably Freda Thorne's mother, the one from the riding school, because she was wearing jodphurs.

'Oh there you are, Elinor dear,' said Auntie Sylvia brightly. Elinor noticed the shifty expression in her eyes: but it vanished as soon as she recognised Elinor's companion.

'Mrs Manaton,' she exclaimed. 'How very nice to see you. Won't you come in? Amy and I were about to have coffee, maybe you'd like to join us – among the packing cases!'

'Welcome to Breadford,' said the tweedy lady, nodding briefly at Mrs Thorne. 'And do call me Sonia. Hello, Amy. No, thank you, I just dropped by with a house-warming gift.'

'Field mushrooms,' deduced Mrs Thorne, sniffing the basket. 'Sonia, you cheapskate.'

'And a suggestion,' continued Mrs Manaton, unruffled. 'I came to see if you could spare young Elinor here for tea, since we missed her back in August. We thought she might like to see some of the things from the big house, as she's interested in local history. That would get one of them out from under your feet, if it would help.'

Auntie Sylvia's eyes glistened. Elinor wondered what had come over her aunt: first calling her 'dear', and now obviously thrilled that Elinor had been invited alone to visit the Rectory. 'How sweet of you. I'm afraid I can't spare Elinor, not today. But Nathalie would love to –'

'Hm,' said Mrs Manaton doubtfully. 'Are you sure? Nathalie was a little bored last time –'

'NATHALIE!' shrieked Aunt Sylvia, sticking her head into the open scullery doorway. 'Oh no.' She hurriedly reverted to her social voice, 'she certainly wasn't bored. Definitely not. Nathalie's very, very keen on antiques. She loves that programme, what's the name, where they guess the auction prices of the *objets*. She'd win a fortune if she was on that. Just a moment. She's been riding this morning, and has gone upstairs to change.'

So it was Nathalie who left, rather sulkily, with the vicar's housekeeper. If Mrs Manaton was annoyed at the swop that had been forced on her she was too polite to show it. Mrs Thorne and Auntie Sylvia moved into the big kitchen-dining room. Freda, who had appeared from upstairs with Nathalie but stayed behind with her mother, gave Elinor a distant smile.

'Hi, Elinor. You don't ride, do you?'

'No,' said Elinor.

End of that conversation.

'Elinor, you'd better go to your room and unpack,' ordered Auntie Sylvia. 'When you've done that, you can check on the children. They're out in the grounds somewhere.'

She didn't mind being sent away. She didn't have a thing to say to Freda, who was one of the most unfriendly members of Nathalie's set. She didn't mind that Nathalie had taken over her invitation, either. She was a little frightened of Mrs Manaton, and the idea of tea with her and Mr Vernon all by herself was overwhelming.

In the back hall she realised that she hadn't asked *which room*? She supposed it would be easy to work out. She'd simply track down her old pine bed, wherever it was. The Dower House was looking strangely confused. Auntie Sylvia had bought some of the old furniture, and it was mingled with newly-arrived Madison possessions. The fox and its withered prey were gone from the front hall, but the hall stand was still there; a Madison rug lying beside it. A Madison carpet was piled in rolls, waiting to be fitted on the front stairs. She went up them, and into the bedrooms that had been shut up. Pale rectangles showed on ancient wallpaper, left by pictures that must have been taken down years ago. A round window looked out on the moor, showing a view she'd never seen before. But the three empty rooms were still empty. One of them, the corner room, was large and square. It had windows west and south that were full of sunset light. She stood on the bare boards, feeling prickled by memory. *I have been here before.*

On the other side of the upstairs door leading to the part of the house they'd rented, a Madison lampshade was lying on the floor, beside a carton of nails and a ball of twine. She found her aunt and uncle's furniture in the master bedroom, and Derek's things in the small room where the bunk beds had been. In the second bedroom,

Megan's suitcases were piled beside one bed. Nathalie's, half unpacked, were strewn across the other. Fittings from the sisters' rooms in the old house were ranged around. The walk-in closet was open and half filled with Nathalie's clothes; cardboard boxes that contained the sisters' other possessions stood in a pile. Elinor stared at this sight, grim realisation dawning.

Everything was the way it had been in the summer. She remembered now, she'd heard Auntie Sylvia say that they were going to *live in the rental part of the house at first.* Until the renovation work was done. Well, that was fine for the Madisons. Elinor didn't happen to mind bare walls, or a bit of damp. She would find out where the removal people had dumped her things, and move herself into one of the empty bedrooms. She wouldn't mind roughing it.

But where were they? Her old pine bed, her suitcases, her desk and wardrobe? She hunted through the house, refusing to consider the obvious answer. Madison sofas and chairs were arrayed in the big front room. The multimedia computer was in the study in its boxes, waiting for Uncle Derek to set it up; likewise the hi-fi equipment. A Madison TV, in spite of the poor reception, was ready to be switched on. Tea-chests were everywhere, full of clothes, crockery, cooking pans, cushions, wastepaper bins, bedside lamps, fruit baskets, tablemats . . .

When she couldn't deny the truth any longer she rushed back to the big kitchen. Auntie Sylvia and Mrs Thorne were sitting with their coffee cups at the Madisons' scrubbed pine table, which was littered with glossy leaflets and swatches of wallpaper material. Freda was boredly trying to build a card house with some paint sample cards. They all looked up, startled.

'Auntie Sylvia, what's going on? Where am I supposed to sleep?'

'Don't be silly dear, you know which is your room. The same as before.'

'I can't sleep in there! Please, *please.* You know I can't!'

Her aunt's chair scraped back with a jerk. 'Excuse me –' she cooed, flashing Mrs Thorne a dazzling smile. 'Teenagers, you know how it is.' In a moment Elinor was out in the hall, the kitchen door shut behind them, her aunt gripping her arm savagely.

'*Elinor*,' she hissed. '*Don't be silly*. You know very well which is your room. If you would *join in* more, you would have been part of the discussion when we sorted everything out. The girls want to share, Dekkie must have a room of his own, and the other bedrooms are not fit to live in. We decided this was the way it had to be, otherwise we couldn't have moved in until the work on the house had been done. That would have taken forever, and it would *not* have been convenient. As for the bed, yours was a disgrace. I don't know why you're creating this fuss. There's nothing wrong with that room. Lots of girls your age would be thrilled. Now *go and unpack*, and don't let me hear another word.'

Elinor felt the blood drain from her face. 'What do you mean, *as for the bed*?'

'It was a disgrace,' said Auntie Sylvia, with that shifty look. 'Now go and unpack.'

There was no sign of the iron doorstop. She wedged the door of the dreadful passage with a fold of cardboard from the unpacking litter, and walked slowly down that narrow way.

The dragon lamp was gone, so were the oak chests. The cheap, tired whiteboard wardrobe from her old bedroom stood against one wall, where the oval mirror had been; her chest of drawers and her shabby bookcase opposite. Her homework desk and her chair stood where the washstand had been. There were no curtains at the windows. Elinor's old curtains lay in a heap on top of the cardboard box into which she'd packed her few private possessions. In the unfamiliar surroundings everything she owned looked sadly battered and worn. But the most battered of her old friends wasn't here.

The fourposter bed stood exactly where it had been before. The same curtains, the same canopy, the same barley-sugar twisted poles. She stared at it, feeling that she had walked waking into a nightmare. She had to go up to the bed and run her hands over it before she was convinced it was real. As she touched the dark wood and breathed the dusty scent of the hangings, all the horror came back.

So now she'd found out why her aunt had been so keen to get her out of the way, Auntie Sylvia knew how much Elinor hated that bed.

And there was the walnut desk, gleaming through a new film of dust, holding its secret. It had a look of bleak satisfaction, as if it was saying: *I knew you'd be back!*

'Why?' wailed Elinor, aloud. 'Why has she done this to me?'

But she forced herself to stay in the room until she heard Mrs Thorne and Freda driving away: steeling herself for a big argument and making resolutions. She would be calm. The Madisons had their own sofa-bed, which they used for occasional visitors in spite of Auntie Sylvia's reservations. It had been put in the study, she'd seen it there. She could sleep on that. All she had to do was explain, sensibly and firmly, how bad she felt. She went to her aunt with the case well worked out.

It was no use. Auntie Sylvia wanted the fourposter and desk as 'features' in the big square room upstairs – which would be both their spare bedroom and her own sanctum when they didn't have visitors. She hadn't noticed these two 'pieces' in the summer, but since then she'd spotted their value. The desk was going to be worth a fortune when it was restored. Meanwhile, her antiques couldn't be kept upstairs in the damp. Since Elinor's bed had been thrown out she was being *allowed*, for the second time, to sleep in the fourposter. Eventually she would have a new divan, but there was no point in buying it yet, not until the fourposter could be moved. Her aunt pretended that it was Elinor who was being unreasonable. She claimed that this was the first she'd heard of Elinor's feelings about the panelled room and its furniture. 'You're the one who's supposed to like old-fashioned things!' she pointed out, triumphantly. 'You *liked* having that room when we were here in the summer,' she lied. 'It was your choice. I remember distinctly. You wanted to be off by yourself, Miss Snooty.'

Elinor soon forgot her resolutions. She cried and pleaded, it made no difference. Auntie Sylvia was like that. Once she'd made up her mind she'd say anything to defend her position, however weak it was. And she would never, ever let anyone persuade her to back down: though you could see in her eyes that she knew she was in the wrong.

When she shut herself out of the Madisons part of the house that night, Elinor didn't feel like crying. She'd wasted enough tears. As she stood in the dim, chilly hall something that Mrs Manaton had said came back to her. Was it true that she'd known about someone called Mistress Deborah Revelle before she had those dreams? Had she read about the Wicked Lady, about eighteenth-century rebuilding plans, about the little boy called Diccon? The idea that even her nightmares were not her own made her feel worse, not better. Some dog-eared leaflets were stacked on the hallstand, left behind when the holiday house had been sold. She picked them up. Local History, Local Celebrities: if she looked through these she might recognise the source of her other world. '*I don't want to know*,' she whispered. She tore up the leaflets, glancing around defiantly as if someone might be spying on her, and stuffed the pieces in a bin-bag of unpacking rubbish that stood at the foot of the stairs.

She searched under the mattress, half in fear and half in hope. Surely someone must have found her treasure. No, the leather purse was still there. She drew it out and opened it. Tarnished silver and honey-coloured amber, they lay on her palm again: the yellow ear-bobs. She stared at them, by the light of her little desk lamp. 'I didn't make it up,' she said aloud. 'Those things happened to me.' Now was her chance to make things right, to return the earrings to their original hiding place and throw away that stupid curse of hers. But she couldn't bring herself to do it. Not tonight.

'*I wanted them*,' she whispered. The hateful atmosphere of the bed closed around her, and she almost welcomed it. She had tried to start afresh, it was no good. Whatever evil lived in the fourposter room, she was in its power. She had been fated to come back. There was no escape.

Six

THE MASTER WAS AWAY IN LONDON. MISTRESS Deborah decided to remove herself and young Diccon from the noise and dirt of the rebuilding, to the pretty little white house that was standing empty a mile down the valley, just within Revelle park. Since she had lost the baby everyone had great sympathy with Mistress Deborah's whims. Her husband had ordered that she must be obeyed in everything while he was gone. No one protested when she took with her only Nelly, one groom and an old woman to do the cooking.

The other servants thought Nelly was unjustly favoured, but the move turned her into a maid of all work. Though part of the little house stayed shut up, the rooms that the Mistress would use had to be scrubbed and burnished and kept in perfect order; it was very hard for such a young girl. And she was frightened. There were things about this move that she didn't understand.

On the surface, all was well. Mistress Deborah wished for quiet and wanted few visitors. She received the vicar, the doctor and one or two of Simon Revelle's female relatives in the bright first-floor chamber she called her 'salon'. Nelly heard her declare that she found 'life in a cottage' charming. She was enjoying, she said, like the French queen, a simple little pastoral . . . Yet once Nelly went into the kitchen and found Mistress Deborah herself, with her sleeves pinned up, hair draggled and cheeks pink, doing her own cooking. She didn't look as if she was playing make-believe. The old woman, Martha Whiddon, was slumped on a chair in the corner, snoring. Nelly had seen enough of life to know she was dead drunk. For that intrusion, Mistress Deborah had given her a sound whipping. She was angry, of course, at being caught doing servant's work. But why didn't she turn Martha away? Why had she brought a cook who was a drunkard to the Dower House? As Nelly now remembered, everyone at the big house knew that Martha was inclined to drink.

Nelly did not play with Diccon any more. He was too old to need a nursemaid. The Mistress kept him with her, except when he went out rambling on his pony. She said she was teaching him his letters, which puzzled Nelly because Diccon already knew 'his letters', and more. He could read Latin, like a clergyman: which Nelly was sure her Aunt Deborah could not do. But often when she had to pass the room she would hear a ringing slap. When she came in to mend the fire or bring the tea tray she saw her former playmate white-faced and weeping. Diccon was having a sorry time over his lessons. She would have pitied him more, except that he was so cold to her. He would hardly look at her or speak, if they met during the day.

She wondered enviously why the Mistress kept him so close, if she didn't enjoy Diccon's company. What had happened to her plan to send the boy to school? If the baby that had been expected had not died unborn, Diccon would have been sent away and Nelly would have been important again; and had a new babe to love. Long ago in the time that seemed so dim now, when she lived at home with Mother, Nelly recalled a woman, a neighbour, who made her living as a wet nurse. Her name was Dorothy. She was old by little Nelly's estimate, with a fat red face. It had been strange to see her with a tiny baby sucking at her breast. She was a good enough woman, mother said. But there were other nurses, *killing nurses* they were called, who would take charge of a baby that some richer folk didn't want: and it was understood they were to let it die. She wondered, ashamed of her own nasty fancies, if there was such a thing as a *killing school.* What if Diccon were sent off and didn't return?

It was March, the beginning of a wet, sunless spring. The master didn't return. He would come back with a title said the servants at the big house, admiring Mistress Deborah's ambition. He would keep from home until the building was done, because he could not bear to see the ruin of the old place, said others. Twice a week Nelly walked the bleak mile from the Dower House with a letter, that would be taken on horseback to the post house in Eaxby. Sometimes the roads were so bad that the letter was bound to lie at Revelle House or at Eaxby for days on end but Aunt Deborah, though she was no great penwoman, never failed. That walk became very long. It was haunted by evil fancies. There was never a living soul to be seen, and the sky was so vast, and the curlews on the moor cried like lost spirits. Sometimes she wished she dared to open the paper she carried and add a secret message to her master, in her own poor lettering: *Come home*! He would save her from herself, from her wicked thoughts. But she did nothing.

Aunt Deborah did not ride, since her pregnancy and its sad ending. When she went to church on Sunday, or when she wanted to inspect the building work, she would dress herself finely and despatch the groom to the big house to have a carriage sent. She scarcely left the house otherwise. But one dark evening Nelly caught her coming out of a room that they called the panelled room, on the ground floor, dressed in a man's clothes. She almost screamed, thinking a highwayman or a smuggler had got into the house. Then she saw her aunt's face in the candlelight: and the cry was stifled in her throat.

In her dashing days Aunt Deborah had sometimes dressed in men's clothes for riding, to the scandalised delight of the whole county. The master had not liked it. There had been a stormy argument, and she'd had to give up her breeches.

'Nelly,' she said, standing there in the cold dark, her eyes very bright. 'You mustn't tell.'

She took Nelly by the wrist, in a grasp so fierce it burned, and drew her away from that little blind passage that led to the panelled room: up the stairs and into her own bedchamber. She sat on the stool by her dressing table, one hand still gripping Nelly, the other laid on the loose white shirt under her open coat.

'Don't tell, Nelly. You must not tell.'

She wouldn't have thought of asking for the ear-bobs. It was Aunt Deborah who offered them. She lifted her fine white hand and reached on to the dressing table, picked out those yellow jewels and dangled them in front of Nelly's eyes. The silver lyres glittered. The drops of amber glowed, a tiny candleflame flickering in each honeyed heart.

'You want them, don't you? You silly girl, I've seen you ogling, like a beggar at the pastrycook's. See, they are always here. I don't lock them away.'

'I won't tell master,' quavered Nelly. 'I won't tell that you wore the breeches.'

Aunt Deborah laughed, and laid the jewels down again. The thought crept into Nelly's mind, sly as a snake, that she had a guiltier secret. Was this why they had come to the Dower House? So that Mistress Deborah could slip out on to the moor, and meet some bold lover? She looked at the jewels hungrily. Mistress Deboarah could not hand them over, not directly. That would have been admitting too much. But Nelly felt there was an unspoken bargain. She was to have the earrings in return for her silence.

'Good girl. Don't you ever say a word.'

In the night as she lay on her truckle bed in a slip of a room above the kitchen, in the back part of the house, she would hear a pattering of feet in the passageway. Diccon would come to her. She would hold him in her arms as she used to in the old days, while he muffled his sobs in the folds of her coarse nightgown. But while she soothed him the devil in her whispered: *why should I pity a gentleman's son*? She thought bitterly how no one, not a soul, seemed to remember now that Nelly was Mistress Deborah's own kin. Her young body ached so she couldn't sleep, from the work of the Dower House. Diccon only had to bear a few light blows and fierce looks. His food was still dainty, his clothes clean and fine. All her life poor Nelly would have nothing more than drudgery and a servant's wage . . .

Elinor opened her eyes and saw a vase full of berries and bracken, standing on the top of her bookshelves. It was November, not March. She remembered that it was a church-cleaning Saturday. Oya, with that talent she so admired for making the best of things, had made good friends with the vicar and his housekeeper. It was Oya's writing she had seen on that notice about the swallows and the screen door. He regularly took his homework to the Rectory where he could work in peace in Mr Vernon's study; and he often turned up for the church-cleaning. He'd promised Elinor that this was more fun than it sounded. Plus there was 'payment in kind' afterwards, in the form of most excellent chunky bacon sandwiches sent over from the Fish. Elinor had agreed to give it a try.

It was two and a half weeks since the Madisons had moved into the Dower House. Two and a half weeks of sleeping in this bed: and no end of the ordeal in sight. The work on the house wouldn't begin until after Christmas. It could be months before it was over. Sometimes the dreams about Nelly seemed like an escape. It was better to dream of drudgery than to lie waiting for that choking fear to begin, the feeling that she was *buried alive* under the horrible canopy, between the hateful curtains . . . She hadn't moved yet. She was lying still, just as she had woken. The dream fogged her mind, as if she was a double-exposed photograph. She could almost feel the child's warm weight in her arms, his hair brushing her chin. A shiver of the nameless dread that haunted the other girl ran through her. It was a dream, she reminded herself. You're making all this up, remember? You read those leaflets, and made up a fantasy about a dead little boy. It must be time to get up. She turned to reach for her clock. *And saw, printed in the sheet and pillow by her side, the hollow made by a child's body.*

She gasped in disbelief. She touched the place: *it was warm*. What child had lain there, *in her arms while she was sleeping*? This time she knew it could not have been Dekkie. He didn't have nightmares now: and if he did there was no way he would have left his room, come downstairs in the dark and trekked all the way to the fourposter room to find Elinor. They were no longer friends. Only last night, he'd given her such a hard time when she was putting him to bed that she'd been nearly crying.

Nelly's voice whispered, in Elinor's mind: '*He is a gentleman's son.*'

She had drawn back as far as possible from that unspeakable, impossible imprint. She stared at it, trembling. 'W-what's happening to me?' she begged. But there was no one to answer. She could not touch the place again. She slipped out of bed and dragged her duvet until it fell on the floor. With her eyes screwed shut and her face turned away she pulled the bedsheet tight. If she'd been able to she'd have opened the windows, as if fresh air could disinfect this room, and take away the sickening fear.

She dressed hurriedly. The Madisons were late sleepers at the weekends, at least she didn't have to deal with them. She took her bike from beside the garage and rode into Breadford. It was the same bike that she'd had in the summer, bearing the battle scars of her fall. She didn't mind this. She'd rather not have a new bike: it would only make Nathalie and Megan angry. When she arrived at St Breada's, Oya was polishing the eagle whose wings supported the reading-desk in the sanctuary. Mrs Manaton and young Mrs Hawk from the Flying Fish were in the North Porch, sorting flowers. Mr Vernon was on a ladder under the organ loft, poking at something in the wall.

'No Nathalie?' remarked Mrs Manaton.

Auntie Sylvia had heard about the church cleaning, and been determined that Nathalie should come and help too. She'd never have considered such an idea in town, but she was convinced that church work was the key to Breadford's best society. She was right about this, in a way: but Nathalie was not impressed. Elinor had forgotten that she was supposed to bring her cousin. It wouldn't have made any difference if she'd remembered. Nathalie was extremely stubborn when it came to getting up on a Saturday morning. She shook her head.

Mrs Manaton sighed. 'People think they want the old-fashioned country ways,' she complained, sizing up some leggy bronze chrysanthemums, 'They don't realise that it means *work*. Not half as bone-crushing or soul-destroying as it once was: but hard manual labour, by modern standards, is still the backbone of the lifestyle people think they want.'

'Townies,' grumbled Mrs Hawk. 'They don't know they're born.'

Mrs Manaton and Mrs Hawk, a brisk young woman with rosy cheeks and a mass of curly black hair, were the core of the cleaning team. Mr Vernon, who was vicar of Eaxby Torent (a tiny village, not the market town), Mixton and Darebridge as well as Breadford, had other churches to worry about. These two were as passionate as a pair of vintage car enthusiasts over St Breada's. They liked nothing better than to spend a whole weekend tinkering with her innards and burnishing her metalwork. What they didn't know about the ancient little gem was not worth knowing. Mr Vernon complained that if they had their way, God and St Breada (the obscure Saxon lady to whom the church was dedicated) would not be allowed into the place, in case they left fingerprints on the brassware.

'Not all townies,' said Mrs Manaton, smiling at Elinor. 'And be fair, Rosie. Maybe they'd miss St Breada's if it suddenly vanished, but most people who've lived here all their lives are never going to scrub bat-droppings from the chancel walls.'

An image from her dreams flashed into Elinor's mind. She was on her knees, cleaning the flagged floor of the Dower House kitchen. Her arms were red to the elbows. Her chilblained feet were itching furiously, in the cracked men's boots she had to wear to get around the muddy yard. She was hungry, cold, and so weary she was crying as she worked . . . A wave of pure rage rushed through her like poison. Suddenly she knew she shouldn't have come here. She turned and almost ran up the aisle. There was Oya, rubbing happily at the eagle's supercilious beak.

'Isn't he looking wonderful? Look at that sheen. Like silk. I never thought I could get this good at polishing. I'm as good as Rosie Hawk now, *and* faster.'

'I think you're wasting your time,' said Elinor. Her voice was shaking. 'I don't know why you let them make you do that. It's drudgery, just *hateful drudgery*.'

Oya stopped work and stared at her. 'Nobody's making me do it. I'm enjoying myself.'

Rosie Hawk, an active young mother who never liked to see a teenager with idle hands if she could help it, had come after Elinor with another can of metal polish and a bundle of rags.

'Come on,' she ordered cheerfully. 'There's the altar bell, and all the candlesticks.'

Elinor's breath hissed between her teeth. 'You can keep them,' she snarled. 'Do it yourself.' She grabbed the can and flung it to the floor, where it rang against a fifteenth-century brass tablet and bounced off between the benches. Mrs Hawk and Oya stared with their mouths open. Elinor rushed away, tears springing.

She meant to run out of the church. But Mr Vernon stood in her way. 'Come and see this, Elinor,' he said quietly.

She followed him back to his ladder, sure there was a scolding coming. But he said nothing about her outburst. 'Look.' He pointed. 'Get up on the ladder, you'll see better.'

There was a ragged hole in the cream washed plaster of the wall under the choir loft, with a big vertical crack on either side. Daylight showed through it. When she climbed up she discovered that the hole was partly blocked by a cup of greyish clay, mixed with straw.

'It was a swallows' nest. So much for my screen door, eh? We had to leave it undisturbed all summer. But then I forgot to organise the repairs: and now look.' The straws that poked out of the cup jerked. A tiny nose appeared, whiskers twitching indignantly. 'Squatters!' groaned Mr Vernon. 'At least they're only fieldmice. If anything endangered had decided to colonise, we'd be sunk. As it is, if they're not out of there in a week I'm going to get ruthless. I'm going to serve a court order, in the form of Rosie's cat. If we don't fix this soon the entire west wall's going to fall apart.'

Elinor was not fooled by the wildlife expert. She came down the ladder and waited. Get it over with, she thought. 'Sometimes family life can be hard,' said Mr Vernon, as if he was continuing a conversation they'd already started. 'Everyone has to compromise. Sometimes the best thing is a little distance. Make space for yourself in your mind: and in your daily life as far as you can. Like me and those mice. I tell myself the situation isn't going to last forever, and I make the best of it.'

Elinor knew that Oya trusted Mr Vernon. The kindly, scatterbrained vicar understood about the MacDonalds. He accepted that Oya didn't want to tell his parents he was having a hard time, and simply did what he could to help. And there was Mrs Manaton, who'd been a vicar's wife in a neighbouring group-parish. She had no children, and no training for any kind of job. She'd been left stranded, penniless and alone when her husband died; until Mr Vernon quietly managed to find the funds to employ a housekeeper. Obviously he thought he understood about Elinor's problems too; and he assumed it was his job to help. Probably everyone in Breadford had discussed the new family at the Dower House, and noticed that Elinor didn't fit in, poor thing. Her cheeks burned at the thought of the pitying gossip.

But Mr Vernon was wrong. They were all wrong. Living with the Madisons, being bullied by her aunt and teased by her cousins, was *nothing* compared with what had happened to her this morning. She looked up at the vicar helplessly, knowing that he saw the face she'd glimpsed in the mirror in the scullery before she came out: hollow-eyed, haggard and desperate. But he wouldn't believe her if she told him why she looked like that. She wished that the ghosts of the fourposter bed were werewolves or skeletons in chains. Oh no, it had to be poor Nelly the nursemaid and her Aunt Deborah, the Wicked Lady. She knew that whatever she said people would think she was *really* talking about how Aunt Sylvia treated her. They'd think she was using the history of the Dower House as a disguise for her own troubles, because she was *an abused child.* Mrs Manaton had practically said that, or something like it, when she'd begun to tell the story of the Wicked Lady. *I can see you know all this already*, she'd said, before Elinor tried to say anything about the ghosts.

She wanted to say, I'm not abused! Auntie Sylvia's not that bad. I can cope. I was managing much better, until we came back here. It's that house, it's that room, it's that horrible bed. It's because of the yellow ear-bobs. But she knew how it would sound. She shook her head.

Mr Vernon patted her on the shoulder, with a wise smile. Like he understood that she would talk when she was ready. 'Brass polishing is too good for you,' he decided. 'I'm going to advise the chiefs of staff to give you a nasty, hard, messy job.'

So Elinor was put in charge of the flowers. She grew calm again, surrounded by autumn-scented chrysanthemums, golden rod and japanese anemones, rusty fronds of bracken and feathery grasses. Samson Brewer, an enormous young man in a big black leather jacket, son of Brewers the Bakers, came into the vestry to fetch the fearsome ancient floor-polishing machine. He was a friend of Joe MacDonald but nothing like a MacDonald in personality. 'It's something to do, innit?' he remarked cheerfully. 'Gets you out of the house.' She nodded, thinking of *that warm hollow in the bedclothes.* She wanted to believe it hadn't been there. Oh please, let it have been her imagination. If only nothing so horrible happened again.

When she'd finished the flowers she was feeling better. Samson was practising the organ now: the music flowed like silk. She gathered up cut stems and discarded leaves in a bundle of damp newspaper and took them out to the compost bin in the churchyard. The sky was dull and the air was chilly. Autumn was fading into winter. A misty rain had begun to fall, it tingled faintly on her cheeks and hands.

Something, maybe a sense that she was being watched, made her look towards the great yew tree. She saw a figure standing in the deep shade beside the Revelle tomb. It was someone wearing a wide-brimmed dark hat, white shirt and a full-skirted coat over jodphurs or breeches: almost like fancy dress. The hat shaded the figure's face, but she felt eyes on her, intently staring. There was something naggingly familiar about that stance, about the gleam of curling fair hair under the hat brim.

Mistress Deborah. It was Mistress Deborah, coming out of the panelled room in a man's riding dress . . . Elinor stood, fear welling up inside until it filled her whole body. She wanted to scream, she wanted to beg the vision to go away. But she couldn't move or speak.

Oya wondered what had got into Lin. It was unlike her to snap like that. He'd often seen her miserable, never angry. She wasn't the type. When he'd finished his polishing he went to look for her. The vestry was empty except for the flowers in their big vases, waiting to be moved to their positions around the church. He looked out into the churchyard and saw her standing with her back to him, so still he thought a deer must have come into the churchyard and she didn't want to startle it.

'Lin? Elinor? What's wrong?'

She turned, slowly. Her cheeks were pinched and grey, her eyes frantic.

'You look as if –' He laughed, trying to make a joke of it. 'I was going to say *you look as if you'd seen a ghost.* Except that wouldn't be much of a shock in here. It's natural ghost territory.'

'I didn't see anything!' wailed Elinor. 'What are you staring at? Leave me alone!'

The churchyard gate clanged. The two little Hawk twins, Jessy and Johnny, came running up the path, followed by their father who was carrying a loaded tray. Oya decided it would be best to pretend that nothing had happened. He raised a cheer for the famous bacon sandwiches. But he was almost sure *he'd* seen something, or someone – a human shadow that had vanished so quickly it had seemed to melt into the rain-blurred shape of the Revelle tomb.

Elinor didn't tell anyone. She knew she mustn't tell. She did what she should have done the first night she came back to the Dower House. She returned the earrings to their hiding place in the desk; and recovered that stupid scrap of paper. It had grown old in the months it had spent in darkness. The yellowed edges crumbled when she spread it out. Nathalie's name and Megan's had faded into the faintest brown scratchmarks. *Harm to them* was just a blur. Only Derek's name was still clear. It was hard to believe that she had actually written this in her own blood. But she remembered every detail of that afternoon, when the Madisons had gone to the cinema and left her locked in the fourposter room. She remembered the injustice of her punishment. She remembered pacing about, trying the windows, her despairing plan to run away and live on the streets. DEKKIE . . . She stared at the brownish scrawled letters, filled with cold fear. She was too frightened to tear the paper up or throw it away, so she hid it between two pages of a school book.

At the end of the week she realised that she had stopped dreaming of Nelly. But on Monday, when Elinor got off the country bus with Oya, the watcher was waiting for her. She saw that same shadow, exactly like Aunt Deborah in her man's dress, standing within the churchyard. Somehow, her heart thumping like a trapped bird inside the cage of her ribs, she managed to say goodbye in a natural tone, cross the street and walk on by. When she dared to look back, it was gone. On Tuesday, Auntie Sylvia was in town to collect them. Elinor came home in the car with Nathalie and Megan. But then her aunt sent her into the village to buy some forgotten groceries. The shadow was waiting, blurred in the halo of the streetlight that stood by the churchyard gate. Next day it was there again . . . pacing in the November dusk: waiting and watching.

She did not dream, but she didn't sleep. Images whirled in her mind as she lay in the terrible bed. Aunt Deborah's brilliant eyes looking out of the shadow. Aunt Deborah coming from the panelled room in the darkness and thin candlelight, with such a frightening expression on her face . . . The yellow ear-bobs, pressed into Nelly's red, chapped hand. The yellow ear-bobs, so beautiful and so wicked. How those jewels had tormented poor Nelly! Sometimes Elinor thought she heard Diccon's pattering footsteps, sometimes she heard the rustling of Mistress Deborah's gown. She refused to open her eyes, so they couldn't make her see. But she understood that returning the earrings had achieved nothing. The watcher in the churchyard was getting bolder. It would catch her in some lonely place. She would be walking down the dark lane to the Dower House alone. There would be footsteps behind her. She would turn and see the ghost. And she would be trapped: nowhere to run but straight to the Dower House, where the heart of the evil lay.

She knew why the dreams had stopped. It wasn't because she had escaped. The story that the dreams had been telling had been broken off unfinished because *she knew all that she needed to know.* That was why the shadow had come. She had made a bargain with wickedness, and it was time to pay the price.

One afternoon, there was a thick fog in town. At the end of school the road outside was invisible. Cars were reduced to a procession of crawling headlights in a murk of grey. Mothers doing the school run came groping up to the kerb, their faces peering anxiously through blurred windscreens. It was one of the days when Nathalie would get a lift with Freda's mum or Caroline's, and Elinor would come back on the bus with Oya. The school bus, a red double-decker that seemed poorly suited to the Breadford and Eaxby route, was driven sometimes by a very careful young man, but sometimes by a stout woman with bushy blonde hair, who sang as she drove and handled the narrow lanes in an audacious, swinging style that had the whole top deck shrieking aloud. It was fun. The children called her Calamity Jane.

Naturally, the fog had made the bus late. Nathalie had left with Freda. Elinor stood in the crowd, which had shrunk to a core of country bus users and a few people whose parents must be trapped in the creeping traffic. Everyone around her was trying to crank up this minor piece of weather into a disaster. People were wondering if they'd ever get home, half-hoping they'd have to sleep in the classrooms, make beds out of school curtains; cook up their supper in the chemistry lab.

'Whip crack away!' yodelled Oya, bouncing up and down and punching the air. He was in high spirits because he had a letter from home. He'd read it once at speed (to make sure the news was all good), and once to enjoy it. He was looking forward to a third, leisurely reading in his bed-cave, with his earplugs and his iron rations. 'Calamity Jane won't let us down!'

But he was watching Elinor carefully. He'd been worried about her all week. She'd been unhappy ever since he'd known her, but since the last church-cleaning Saturday she'd been *different* and he didn't like it. She'd always been shy and quiet. Now it was as if she was in another world. He saw her stiffen, and felt her sharp indrawn breath.

'What is it?' he demanded.

She had seen the watcher. The figure appeared to be standing at the edge of the crowd of schoolchildren, ignored by everyone. She couldn't tell Oya. There was no point in telling him. No one else could see what Elinor saw. But there was no mistake. It was the same apparition as she had seen pacing in the shadows by the Revelle tomb: a slim dark blur in the thickened air, invisible eyes staring with relentless meaning. The chattering voices seemed to draw away from her. Her world had nothing in it but the shadow, that watched her silently. She knew she mustn't look that way but she couldn't help herself. She saw the figure move, as if coming towards her. 'No!' she wailed, and ran out into the road.

'*Hey*!' yelled Oya. 'Don't!'

Horns blared as Elinor dodged through the fog-bound traffic. She reached the far side and kept on, not caring which way she was going, pelting along the greasy damp pavements, down an underpass and up into the streets again, ducking umbrellas and veering away from startled, scarf-wrapped faces, skidding around slick plastic-aproned baby buggies. She dived into the nest of narrow alleys where tourists thronged in summer and finally stumbled into the shallow bowl of turf that surrounded the Cathedral.

She reached the great north doorway, her breath burning

in her throat and her legs shaking. She hadn't headed this way on purpose. She didn't think the big church was a safe haven. The ghost had come to find her at St Breada's, it was not afraid of holy ground. But at least there'd be no fog inside. She'd be able to see what was following her. There weren't many visitors on this winter's day. She dared to glance behind her.

'Lin!'

The shadow had not followed her, but Oya had.

'You've got to tell me,' he insisted, coming up to her in the transparent gloom, still trying to catch his breath. 'You can't pretend there's nothing wrong. What scared you?'

Elinor walked away. He followed.

'Do you believe in ghosts?' she whispered. Over their heads, in a glass case, hung Captain Robert Falcon Scott's sledge flag, from the expedition before the one when he reached the South Pole and died on the way back. Oya had told Elinor about it, it was one of his favourite relics. She couldn't understand the attraction. Oya thought of the great adventure. Elinor could only think of the explorer's tragic death.

'I'm not sure,' he said, taking the question perfectly seriously. 'I don't think I've ever seen one. But maybe you wouldn't know, not necessarily. A ghost could just look like a person.'

'You won't believe me if I tell you. You'll think I'm going mad. *She comes for me.* No one else can see her. She's come for me because I took the yellow ear-bobs, I made a bargain and I have to keep it, that's why she's following me.'

'But I did,' said Oya.

Elinor stared at him. 'What?'

'I saw her. Actually I thought it was a man, a thin man in a dark coat and a big hat. Sort of out-of-place looking, but definitely there. I'm pretty sure I've seen him before, too, hanging around in Breadford. This is serious. It could be you've picked up a stalker, some kind of creep who likes harrassing children. You've got to tell someone. People like that are dangerous.'

Elinor shook her head.

'No. It's not that, Oya. I can't explain, but I *know*. It wouldn't do any good to tell.' *Don't tell!* whispered Mistress Deborah's voice in her mind. *Don't ever tell!*: and she shuddered. 'Believe me, it's not some playground creep. *It's not a living person.*'

A shiver ran down Oya's spine, the hair on the back of his neck bristled. He was not sure of what he had seen. All he really remembered was a strong impression of someone staring like a hungry animal, like one of the MacDonalds' horrible dogs.

'If you won't, then I will,' he warned her. 'You can't go on like this.'

'No!' she cried, suddenly loud: so that the few cathedral visitors all jumped and looked their way. 'Please don't! Oya, promise me you won't. I swear to you, *I know who's following me*, and it's not what you think. You mustn't, mustn't ever tell!'

Oya argued, but in the end he had to promise. It was the only way he could get her to calm down. They left the fluted pillars under Scott's flag together and headed back to school. He would have liked to hold her hand, or her arm, to make sure she didn't run away again. But she looked so wretched and reckless he was afraid she'd just gallop off like a wild pony if he touched her. Luckily for them Calamity Jane had counted heads, and their bus was still waiting by the gates when they got back. 'Fine time to go sightseeing!' she lectured them. 'Aren't we late enough for you? I ought to report this.' But she liked Oya and Elinor. They were good-mannered ones, who'd never given her any trouble before. She let them off with a warning.

Oya, as he lay in bed that night with his precious letter, racked his brains for a way to help. The problem was, he couldn't bring himself to betray her trust. She seemed so alone. He tried to imagine what life would be like if we didn't have a family. No mother and father, no grandma, no brothers and sisters. No home. He'd thought that he was being very brave about being sent to school in England, but Elinor's plight was much worse. *I'm going to have to do something*, he thought. He couldn't quite believe it was a ghost he had seen. But whether the stalker was a real nasty person or something worse, Elinor definitely needed help.

Seven

ELINOR LAY VERY STILL IN THE FOURPOSTER BED. She had been crying but that was over now. It was late at night, the Dower House was very quiet. She felt as if she had been lying here for years. Ahead of her, by a light that came from nowhere, she seemed to see a long, dim passageway, maybe one of those long creaking and rambling passages in the old Revelle Manor, that had stood for so many hundreds of years before it was knocked down to make way for Mistress Deborah's new mansion. Coming towards her she saw the figure of a girl: a small, thin girl with a timid, humble expression, wearing a long dress made of some kind of rough grey wool, her brown hair mostly hidden under a white cap. The servant-girl was walking very carefully, as if she was carrying something heavy. She was bringing something to Elinor, who lay in the closed trap of the fourposter bed. Elinor could not move, though she felt a stifling pressure of horror as the girl drew near. She was still lying on the bed, but it seemed as if she was meeting the other girl, face to face. She looked into poor Nelly's bewildered and despairing eyes as if she was looking into a mirror. Something in her cried silently *No! No! Leave me alone!* But though Nelly was so weak and simple, her power over the person who lay in that bed was invincible. And the two girls merged into one.

The ghosts were real now. Elinor could not escape from

the nightmares by waking. At school she couldn't pay attention. At home she walked around the Dower House in a daze, seeing things that weren't there. Instead of fitted carpets and gleaming tiles she saw the uneven floors of waxed wood and flagged stone that she had scrubbed and polished. Instead of electric lamps she saw the silver candelabra that were so hard to clean; and the dark old-fashioned furniture from King James's day that Mistress Deborah so disliked. When she passed the doors of the garage where Uncle Derek's car stood beside the Espace, she heard Diccon's pony moving restlessly in the stable. When she looked up the front stairs she saw the whisk of Mistress Deborah's bright morning gown, going through the door of her 'salon'. When she went out of doors she shambled as she walked, because in Nelly's world she was wearing men's boots stuffed with straw to combat the springtime mud.

It no longer made her angry when Nathalie and Megan teased her. They were the daughters of the house, she was the poor relation. They had the right. She scraped her hair back and wore her drabbest clothes. It seemed more in keeping with her station. When Auntie Sylvia scolded her or hit out in irritation, she hung her head and muttered, 'Yes, m'am, I beg pardon ma'am,' in a voice that wasn't like her own.

Even her aunt noticed that there was something wrong. 'Don't *slouch* like that, Elinor!' she would snap. 'What are you staring at all the time? Really, you look half mental.'

Every night she took out that scrap of scrawled paper from its hiding place, but she couldn't bring herself to destroy it. She was afraid of the ghosts' vengeance. She took out the yellow ear-bobs and looked at them. She had cleaned the silver until it glowed, hoping that this might appease the spirits. They only looked more wicked, though they were still so beautiful. She stood in the light of her desklamp, staring at herself in the small mirror that stood on her chest of drawers. She didn't dare to put them on, but she held the ear-bobs to her ears and turned her head to and fro, in reluctant fascination. The face in the mirror wavered and changed. It was the face of the other Elinor, poor Nelly. The evil that inhabited that panelled room was taking over. *She was turning into Nelly*. She was becoming possessed by the spirit of a long-dead servant girl: and she knew that worse lay ahead. But she could not break free.

And then, one day in school, she remembered that long-ago conversation with Mr Vernon. Putting the earrings back in the walnut desk had done her no good. But what if she could find out who they really belonged to, and give them back to a living person? Mr Vernon, 'the last representative of the old family' had said he didn't have anything to do with the Revelle property. And that suited Elinor, because she still didn't want to tell her story to Mr Vernon. But there must be *someone*. Her aunt and uncle must know. They must have bought the Dower House from somebody who owned it, not just from the estate agents. The idea was a revelation, a glimpse of actual hope!

After school that day, she couldn't resist snatching her first chance to find out. She was preparing the evening meal for herself and her cousins. Auntie Sylvia was perusing her cookery books, of which she had a large and glossy collection, looking for a suitable recipe for her contribution to the Carol Singers' Buffet Supper. Christmas was coming, and having discovered that the Carol Singers' Buffet was a vital engagement on the local festive calendar, Auntie Sylvia had made sure she enlisted herself and Nathalie and Megan in the Four Parishes Carol Choir. Elinor was always nervous when her aunt was in the kitchen with her. Auntie Sylvia had a habit of ordering her to do something else, at a crucial stage in the cooking, so that the vegetables boiled dry or the pasta was overcooked to slimy mush. Her anxiety made her think of the maids in Revelle House who used to pester Nelly: but she fought the waves of nightmare unreality, and kept her mind on the questions she needed to ask.

'Auntie Sylvia, who did you buy the house from? Was it from some connection of the Revelles?'

'No it wasn't. Apparently the family died out years ago.'

This was still a sore point with Auntie Sylvia, who had felt cheated when she discovered that 'the Revelles' no longer existed.

'But then who did the Dower House belong to? If, if we found anything they'd left.'

Elinor was putting together ham salad, to be followed by swiss roll and custard, Dekkie's top favourite dessert. She was glad it was an easy supper. Her school work was suffering because she couldn't concentrate. There was going to be trouble soon. Her aunt and uncle would hear about the homework that was never done, the inattention in class. She was hoping that tonight she'd be able to get enough work done to delay the inevitable reckoning.

'We dealt with a financial company, if it is any of your business.' Auntie Sylvia's temper suddenly flared. 'Anything found in this house belongs to us, you cheeky girl. Why are you asking all these questions?'

'I just wondered. I'm sorry.' Elinor, trembling, started to break eggs into a bowl.

'What are you doing now? I thought I told you to make some custard!'

'The eggs are for a custard, ma'am,' she faltered.

'You *stupid girl!* There's custard powder in the store cupboard, if there's none of the frozen packs left. Look at that waste, a whole half dozen eggs!' Aunt Sylvia could not see the shadows of another world and time. She slapped Elinor – maybe rather harder than she'd meant to, catching her a ringing blow across the ear.

'I beg pardon 'm, I'm surely sorry m-m-m –'

'Oh, don't put on that hang dog act! What's the idea of calling me "ma'am"? *Are you trying to be sarcastic*? Let me tell you, you ungrateful little minx, I won't stand for it. *Look at me when I'm talking to you*!'

Elinor was shaking. For a moment the whole present-day world had vanished, it had been terrifying. But she couldn't explain, she didn't dare to try. Her aunt grabbed for the bowl of eggs, and dropped them. The bowl crashed to the floor, bringing the chopping board, the salad bowl and the platter of ham down with it. Elinor stared at the glutinous mass on the red floor tiles, sickened.

'Clear up that filthy mess,' said her aunt coldly. 'There's more ham in the fridge. Divide it between three. Since you've wasted all those eggs as well, *you* can make do with bread and cheese. And I mean the sandwich slices. *Not* your uncle's good cheddar.'

Maybe it wasn't surprising that the world of Elinor's nightmares was getting confused with her daytime reality. Maybe it was true that she was an abused child, taking refuge in fantasy. She wondered what Auntie Sylvia's new friends would think, if they could see the normal routine experience of the Madisons' unwanted extra child. She knew that her aunt never worried about the way she treated her niece, any more than Megan or Nathalie worried about the way they jeered and teased. Elinor was there to be bullied. It was a habit. She thought her Uncle sympathised a little. But if Elinor wasn't licensed prey then *he'd* have to bear the brunt of his wife's bad temper – or else do more to keep her happy. He was too lazy to fancy that.

She cleared up the mess and prepared more salad, feeling dizzy and far away. She should have waited and asked Uncle Derek, who rarely lost his temper: but he probably wouldn't have given her any more of an answer. And now the idea that she could escape from her fate seemed thin and frail. But she would still try. She would go into Eaxby and ask at the estate agents. Since they'd sold the house, surely they'd have to know who had owned it before.

Saturday morning came. She had been awake most of the night, but had fallen into an uneasy doze at last. It was late, past ten, when she woke again. She dressed, mechanically, in the same drab shapeless skirt she'd worn all week; a limp dull blouse and jumper and thin tights. It was getting hard to remember to vary her clothes. Poor Nelly had only one winter gown . . . The Madisons were still in bed, having a comfortable weekend lie-in. There was no church cleaning today. No one wanted her except maybe Oya, and she didn't want to talk to him. He asked too many questions. But it was getting late. She'd better go, before any of the Madisons stirred. She was about to leave, when she suddenly realised that she couldn't cycle to Eaxby in this outfit. She'd freeze. She changed into warm stretch jeans, thick slouch socks, and pulled a big maroon and orange sweater over her head. The girl in the mirror looked extraordinarily different. The sweater had been given to Nathalie by her grandmother. Nathalie thought the colour and pattern ridiculous and had contemptuously dumped it on Elinor. But today the deep and rather garish shades gave a burnish to Elinor's pale olive complexion and brightened her eyes. She remembered, with a cruel pang, all her resolutions to be strong and to change her miserable life. Maybe there was a chance.

It was nearly lunchtime when she reached the little town and left her bike locked up in the empty tourist car park. Taking the earrings with her in her bike bag, she headed for the High Street. The sky was a cold leaden mass, pressing down hard on the church tower, the market cross, the jumbled roofs and chimneys and the brown and purplish moors. She found the estate agents without any difficulty. Davitt and Dareton. She remembered the day in July, when the Madisons had first arrived here. They had stopped the Espace, and Auntie Sylvia had gone in to get the keys. Auntie Sylvia, pleased to be renting a holiday home with such classy social connections, had reported that Revelle House itself was up for sale. She had talked half-seriously about going to look at the place, and been very annoyed when Uncle Derek had flat-out refused. Elinor stared at the ranks of photographs of country properties for sale and rent. It was such a short time since July, but she had lived years: *since she came to Revelle House, to be Master Diccon's nursemaid . . .*

Shuddering, fighting for control of her own mind, she tried the door. But there were no lights inside, and nobody at the desks. It was Saturday, the estate agents had shut at noon.

Elinor walked quickly back up the street to the car park. The little town was as busy as it would ever be, on a winter weekend. People were looking at her. They'd seen her rattling at the estate agents' doors, they wanted to know why. She'd been drawing attention to herself. It didn't take much, in the country. People were not always friendly or always kind, but they were always *interested.* The woman at the check-out in the tiny supermarket in Breadford gave Elinor advice about what to buy, and ordered her not to bother with the expensive products. *The own brand is just as good*, she'd say. *Don't be taken in!* Elinor had never had the heart to explain that Aunt Sylvia would be disgusted at the idea. The car park wasn't empty any more, but it wasn't crowded. She made straight for her bike.

'Another day,' she said aloud, as if she was trying to convince someone. 'I'll try again.'

But she knew she would not. She reached into her bag and took out the earrings. Her fingers seemed to tingle as she touched the leather pouch: it felt like soft, withered human skin. Clutching it, she stood with her back against the wall by the bike rack, feeling both hot and shivery. She wanted to cry. She had tried, and tried, and tried to escape. She had tried to be a different person. But everything she touched went wrong. What if she managed to find out who had the right to the Revelle's property now? Suppose the people at that financial company wanted to know why she hadn't handed the earrings over before? She'd tell them she wasn't a thief, but they wouldn't believe her. She was the poor relation, the outsider, the scapegoat. Everyone would believe the worst.

She felt dizzy. Her knees gave way under her, and she slid into a crouching position, her back pressed against the wall. It had been a mistake to come to Eaxby, she had not escaped from the ghosts here. She could feel them all around. She dug into her jeans pocket and brought out her purse. She'd started carrying the hateful curse-paper everywhere with her, folded up small. She'd become afraid that if she left it in the panelled room the Madisons would find it. She glanced around. Two people who'd come into the car park laden with shopping looked at her strangely.

She waited until the couple had loaded up their car and driven away. Then she unfolded the scrap of paper, with shaking hands. There was absolutely nothing left of the words 'Nathalie' or 'Megan' now. Dekkie's name was still clear and dark. Why didn't it fade? Would it never fade?

Her heart thumped, but she felt stronger here than in the panelled room. At least she could do *something*. She had some matches with her. In her pathetic hope about the estate agents she'd imagined herself simply handing the earrings over: (I found these, I think they belong to one of your clients), then she'd planned to burn the curse and walk away free. Stupid to hope . . . But she would get rid of some part of her torment. She turned to face the wall, the curse-paper on the ground in front of her. Her hands were trembling so much that the first match wouldn't strike. It broke. She took out another. 'I didn't mean it,' she chanted under her breath. 'I won't do what you want! Leave me alone!'

'Lin? *Lin?* Is that you? What are you doing?'

It was Oya. He was looking over the waist-high wall of the car park, peering down at her. She jumped up, crushing the fragments of burning paper under her foot.

'Nothing.'

Oya's eyes went round, then he shrugged. 'I'm doing nothing too,' was all he said. 'Simply had to get out of the house. It isn't any colder out here than it is in my bedroom.'

There was a grey tinge in his dark skin, his shoulders were hunched and his hands thrust deep in his jacket pockets. He seemed to grow smaller as the weather grew colder, as if his whole body was shrinking into itself. *Look at it this way*, he'd told her. *My idea of normal temperature starts where yours ends. A summer day in a heatwave in England barely feels reasonable to me.* For Oya the English winter was an expedition to Antarctica. He might not survive.

'I could just about stand us a couple of hot chocolates at the Hunnipot,' he suggested.

She didn't protest. Both of them knew that she was always broke. She climbed over the wall and they began to walk up the street. Eaxby stood high in Oya's Dartmoor Cake Crawl league. This was an imaginary challenge he had invented: the rule would be that you must consume one hot drink and one bun or cake at each establishment. Eaxby boasted twenty-seven assorted tea shops, cafes, bistros and hotels-that-did-teas. Twenty-eight if you counted the non-profit-making weekly coffee morning at the Friends Meeting House. Oya dreamed of the heroic, record-breaking cake crawl he and Elinor would make, one fine day when he had the money. Meanwhile the Hunnipot, though not the best place for cakes, had the advantage that the hot chocolate came with squirty cream at no extra charge.

They walked in silence. Oya badly wanted to know what Lin had been doing when she'd jumped up, and what it was that she'd stuffed into the bike bag she was now clutching, with such a furtive, frightened look. He'd pretended to notice nothing. He knew he mustn't ask straight out. She seemed better than she'd been looking at school. At least she'd changed her clothes. But she still had those desperate eyes, and he could see she was biting her lips.

'Do you believe in witchcraft?' she asked.

'Huh?' He was taken aback. First ghosts, now witchcraft.

'It's for a project,' Elinor hurriedly explained. 'Folklore, charms, magic, that kind of thing. I need to find out about it. It's for school.'

Oya stopped, delighted. 'Oh, *that* sort of witchcraft! Well, as it happens I do! I never told you about my dad.' (He tried to resist talking about his family, because she had none). 'He used to be an anthropologist. He was a Professor at the University in Fo, that's our capital city, until he had to take a job in the government after our revolution. Look, do you really need information about local folklore? If you do, I've found somewhere amazing. Come on, I'll show you. It's only open at weekends in winter.'

The Hunnipot was forgotten. He led her by the Market Cross and the Bridewell, through the tiny silent garden of St Michael's churchyard where the Angel of Peace presided over the roll of Eaxby's war dead, across the river by the old main road and into a courtyard behind the Swan Hotel. The buildings around this yard were Grade I medieval tumbledown, untouched by any kind of restoration. They housed a rambling Folklore and Local History Museum.

'It's a bit of a mess,' he explained apologetically. 'It needs a proper going-over. Some of the exhibits are feeble, and most of them are falling apart. But it has some *great* stuff.'

There was no one at the desk in the tiny lobby. Oya left two twenty ps (half price entrance fees) on the blotter; and they went in. They seemed to be completely alone. Oya immediately began to point out his favourite treasures: ancient farm tools, primitive mining equipment, town records, yellowing photographs of forgotten country rituals.

Elinor couldn't see what was interesting about a rotten old hoe, or a study of smocking patterns through the ages. The stone-age relics looked like lumps of mud, the stuffed animals were creepy. But she followed him around the rooms, glad that his enthusiasm meant she didn't have to talk. She didn't know why she'd blurted out that stupid question, '*Do you believe in witchcraft?*'. She didn't want to tell Oya what she'd done, or tried to undo. The leather purse in her bike bag was a weight on her mind. All she wanted to do now was get back to the Dower House and hide the earrings again.

'Look at this,' breathed Oya, poring over a flat-topped

glass display cabinet. Elinor peered at a collection of old books. One of them was opened at an illustration of some strange, half-human figures. 'The green man and the corn man,' declared Oya. 'See that guy dressed up in a suit of cornstalks? Apparently someone dressed like that used to walk the Breadford parish boundaries every year, to ward off demons and make the fields fertile. They'd keep the straw from the last sheaf of the harvest, and use it to make his suit every spring. Then at Hallowe'en the suit was burned, but they moved that part to bonfire night after Guy Fawkes became famous. The last suit ever made was preserved and given to the museum. But the curator told me they had to throw it out, because the mice ate it to bits.'

Elinor stared at the faded ink drawing. The corn man looked something like the straw man in the Wizard of Oz, but with the straw stalks on the outside instead of used as stuffing. A memory crept into her unwilling mind. '*I have seen him*,' she whispered. She saw the bare fields, the little children clutching primrose posies. She had brought Diccon to see the straw-man, his hand was tightly clinging to hers . . .

'Have you?' Oya was excited. 'An actual corn man suit? Where was it? In a museum?'

She shook her head. 'I don't remember.'

He looked at her in disbelief. 'You *must* remember where you saw something as cool as that. But anyway the unbelievable, great thing is that we have *exactly the same thing in Asabaland!* I kid you not. If you come to Fo you could see one of these cornstalk suits in the foyer of the Gerard Museum. It's maize or millet with us, not wheat, but everything else is the same. I told my dad. They don't have a photocopier in this place so I drew a copy of the picture myself. He was really interested. You know, I wish you could meet my dad. I'm sure you'd like him.

And my mum. They're not like some grown-ups. They don't live on another planet.'

She backed away from the case, shaking. She hated Oya. She felt as if he'd brought her here on purpose to torment her. They'd reached what amounted to the Folklore Museum Gift Shop. She bumped into a counter laden with cute Dartmoor recipe cards, reprinted chapbooks and pamphlets: old folk songs, small press rural memoirs. She began to pick things up, trying to pretend there was nothing wrong. But the traditional recipes frightened her. They made her think of the drunken cook in the Dower House kitchen.

'*Why don't you tell them?*'

'What do you mean? I just said, I told my dad all about the corn man.'

'If you get on with them so well, why don't you tell them you hate being sent away?'

Oya was brought down to earth. He'd been very relieved when she said she needed information for something at school. At last, he'd thought, a problem that he could deal with. Showing her the Folklore Museum had seemed like such a good idea. At least she'd be able to do her homework. But when they'd reached the museum, he guiltily realised, he'd forgotten about Elinor and been swept away by his own enthusiasm. He simply loved this place.

'I can't. I told you why.' He came to join her at the bookstall, feeling that she'd accused him of being happy when she was miserable. That wasn't fair. It was just that he tried not to let things get him down. 'We're not rich. Don't get that idea. I think I'd hate a proper boarding school worse, but I'm at our school and boarding with the scummy MacDonalds because it's the cheapest way. I can't tell them it's not working. I have to stick it out. It's a question of pride.'

'Yeah. Your dad's pride. If they really loved you they wouldn't do this to you.'

If there was any heating on in the Museum, Oya hadn't noticed it. He felt cold, bone cold. He stared at the uneven flooring, shoulders hunched. He loved his parents so dearly. But while loving them he had to accept that to his daddy a child was a child. A child did not have the rights of an adult, did not have any say in the way his life was planned. And Mummy wouldn't argue. She'd accept whatever Grandma and Daddy said was right. No discussion, no choice. *Oya, you're going to school in England.*

Elinor sighed. 'I'm sorry. I shouldn't have said that. Don't know what got into me.'

'S'all right. Don't worry. I understand.'

They stood side by side, Oya staring at the floor and Elinor absently turning over leaflets, joined by the invisible bond of suffering. Silence, endurance: no escape. Finally Oya said, 'Okay, you've put up with my boring museum. Let's go and get that hot chocolate.'

She didn't respond. She had started to read one of the historical reprints. Oya took another slim paperback from the same pile. 'Hey, it's about your house! It's about the Revelles, and the Wicked Lady –'

'*In the year seventeen eighty-eight,*' he read, '*Tragedy struck the Revelles, Breadford's most prominent local family. One day in March Richard Revelle, aged seven years, went out riding on his pony. The child had been strictly forbidden to leave the confines of Revelle Park, but his pony was found the next day straying on a stretch of moorland notorious for sucking-holes, old mineshafts; and as a haunt of the Black Fly Brothers, a ruthless gang of smugglers. Searchers combed the moor, dragged the lake at Revelle Manor, plumbed all known mineshafts. No sign of the child was found. But suspicious circumstances began to emerge. A farmer gave evidence that he had seen Richard Revelle's pony, a distinctive grey, from a distance on the day he went missing, but he was sure the rider had not been a small child. The boy's riding boots, hat and a new riding crop of which he was very proud were found hidden in the stable of the Dower House, where the boy was living with his step-mother during rebuilding work at the Manor.*

Gradually doubts fell on the maidservant, Elinor or Nelly Gipping, who had formerly been Richard's nursemaid. Mistress Deborah Revelle (our famous "Wicked Lady") revealed that she had missed a pair of silver and amber earrings. She had not challenged Nelly with the theft, being fond of the girl; but the former nursemaid was the only person likely to have taken them. Also, everyone agreed that Nelly had become sullen and distracted in her manner since Diccon's disappearance. Suspicion turned to accusation. It was noted that the wretched girl pleaded her innocence in such terms – "I didn't do it!" – as suggested that she knew some grave harm had come to the child, whereas the search had found no definite evidence of his fate. She was arrested, and held for questioning at Eaxby Courthouse. The charge was that she had stolen a pair of amber earrings, that the child Richard Revelle had discovered the theft, and she had then murdered Richard Revelle in fear that he would betray her.

The crime, so shocking in a young girl, made her briefly famous. A report of her questioning and her behaviour in custody was produced by a local printer. She repeatedly denied her guilt, but in such confused and desperate terms that she was not believed. Did Nelly Gipping kill the child she had nursed? We will never know. She died in custody before she came to trial. The amber earrings were not found. Nor was the body of poor little Richard Revelle. What follows is a facsimile of the locally-printed account of the affair –'

Oya turned the page. The story had caught his attention, but the copy of the actual record was in cramped old black-letter print, and difficult to read. 'I bet she didn't do it. I bet the police or whatever they were called then were the same as they are now. The Revelles were lords of the manor. The police wanted to look as if they were giving the case priority, so they picked on a poor servant and stuck it to her. I bet that was it. Let's go, I'm freezing. It'll be warm in the cafe.'

'I didn't do it,' she whispered hoarsely.

He wished he hadn't brought her here. It was just his luck that she'd happened to pick up a leaflet about a historical tragedy involving another girl called Elinor. But when Elinor was around, it seemed there were ghosts everywhere you turned. ''Course you didn't. It was more than two hundred years ago.' He took the pamphlet from her, turned it face down and shuffled the whole pile of them out of sight. He forced himself to grin cheerily. 'You have a top alibi. You were in the future. They can't pin anything on you. Let's get out of here.'

'I didn't know they said I'd murdered him,' Elinor protested, her voice shaking. 'I knew, I mean I guessed she, I, must have taken the earrings. I knew the little boy had disappeared. But I didn't know the rest. I didn't kill anyone! You won't believe me, but that's true, it's true!'

'I have no idea what you're talking about,' said Oya, beginning to be frightened. He took her arm. 'Come on. Calm down.'

'Oya, I didn't do it. *Please, please, I didn't do it! No, no, I swear to God I didn't do it!*' Her voice had changed. She didn't try to pull away, but she seemed to melt in his grip. She collapsed, huddled in a flinching bundle with her arms around her head as if to fend off blows.

'Oh, don't tell,' she cried. 'Don't tell, don't tell, don't tell, DON'T TELL!'

Oya had never seen anything so eerie or so scary in his entire life. If he hadn't kept a tight hold on himself he might have run away. He had a terrible, horrifying sense that it wasn't his friend crouching there. It was someone else. With an effort, he managed to pull himself together. She was having a panic attack, he had to keep his head. He knelt beside her. 'Hey, Lin it's me, Oya. Are you okay?'

She took a deep breath, and drew her hands away from her face. 'Lin,' she said. As if she'd never heard the name before. 'That's you,' Oya reminded her. 'Lin Madison. Also known as Lin O'Falloren. O'Falloren is your mother's name. That's what you're going to call yourself when you grow up.' The person he knew seemed to come back into her grey eyes. She took the stringy old tissue he was offering to her, and blew her nose.

'It's okay. I'm all right now. It just . . . that story hit me hard where it hurts.'

'Yeah,' agreed Oya. 'Poor Nelly.'

They stood up. She managed a wavering smile. 'I'm all right, honest.'

'Yeah, but Lin you really, really have to talk to someone. What about the counselling at school?' Her eyes went crazy-wide again. 'Okay, okay. You don't want to do that. Calm down, calm down. What about Mr Vernon? Or Sonia, I mean Mrs Manaton? They'd understand, they'd be able to help, I'm sure.'

She shook her head. Her long fine brown hair, with its almost silvery highlights, had come loose and flew in thick strands around her face. 'No,' she said stonily. '*I'm all right*. Don't tell anyone, please. I trust you, Oya. You're the only friend I've got. Swear you won't tell.'

'Well, okay. But –'

'Swear!'

He heaved a sigh. 'I swear I won't tell,' he pronounced, reluctantly. 'I won't tell, *as long as nothing like this happens with you again*. Is that fair?'

She nodded. 'I suppose so.'

Oya though he ought to take her straight home. But he didn't know what good it would do to take her back to the

Madisons. So they walked around the cold streets, while she pulled herself together. This was a worrying experience. He could see that his friend was trying hard to act normal, but she was in a daze. She hardly spoke, and seemed to be looking at a world that he couldn't see. Once she said, 'I burned the curse, Oya. I think I gave it more power. Whatever I do turns out wrong.' But when he asked her what she meant she stared blankly, seeming not to remember what she'd just said.

They ended up at the Hunnipot after all, where Oya sat watching while she bravely pretended to enjoy her drink; while he wondered what on earth he should do next.

Eight

Oya had mentioned in his letters to his parents, that his friend Lin was not happy living with her father's relatives. He didn't think this was betraying any secrets. He had also hinted powerfully that he would like to invite Lin home with him. Giving her a break from the Madisons still seemed to him the best and maybe the only way he could help: and he would *love* to have someone from his English life come to Africa, to knit the two places together. When he'd dropped this heavy hint he'd known it was probably hopeless. Someone would have to pay for her air ticket, and that was a lot to ask: too much to ask from his own parents and definitely too much to expect from the Madisons. But they had not said 'no'. After that day in Eaxby he felt that things had become really urgent. She desperately needed a break. She had no other family, she'd told him that. It would be wonderful if he could suddenly tell her that she could come to Africa for Christmas. Oya, ever-hopeful, decided to call and ask his parents straight out.

He didn't often phone home. He couldn't bear to do it from the MacDonalds' house. Their phone was in the narrow front hall, and they would stand and listen, with their thick pallid tombstone faces expressionless, like a pair of ogres. Maybe they were afraid he was going to complain about the food, or the lack of heating. He preferred tapes or letters. A letter was the best. It was something you could hold on to. On the phone or on a tape cassette those familiar voices sounded so much further away than when he read their words, and heard them speaking in his mind.

He went over to the Rectory to do his homework on Monday evening, and asked Mr Vernon if he could call Asabaland. Of course he was allowed. Mr Vernon's study was a cosy room with bookcases round the walls, a pair of shabby red armchairs in front of the fireplace, and a huge polished table heaped with parish papers. Mr Vernon would cheerfully clear a corner when Oya came to work, shoving documents and leaflets and letters into jumbled tottering cliffs: 'like parting the Red Sea,' he'd remark. Oya, who liked to keep things shipshape, used to look on the mess with horror. But the paper mountain was bound to build up, said Mr Vernon, when you had to keep track of four parishes. The vital thing was to keep calm, and do whatever seemed most pressing.

Mrs Manaton wrote him 'to do' lists that said things like CHANCEL ROOF GUTTERING AGAIN or HOSPICE CAROL-SINGING DATE PLEASE! They lay on top of the clutter and gradually sifted downwards, to become fossilised in the lower strata.

Oya called the international operator and arranged to be told the price of the call so he could pay it at once. He had no trouble getting through. In a few moments Eloise, their maid, answered the phone. She exclaimed with delight at hearing him: and then his mother's voice sang out to him across those hundreds of miles, sweet and wonderful. It was much harder to get them to understand why he was calling. His family, including Fariq the driver, Eloise, his two brothers, his little sister and even his baby sister – who couldn't actually talk – seemed to pile up round the phone at the other end, all wanting a turn. Then there was Grandma, questioning him with fake sternness about his school-work. At last he got his mother back.

'Mummy, what about that idea I had of asking my friend Lin to stay?'

'Oya, why don't you call more often? You don't have to worry about the money too much, it's so good to hear your voice. Are you well? Are you eating well? Have you had a cold?'

'I *am* cold, of course I am, it's practically snowing right now. Not in the room, I mean, but outside. But I'm not sick. Look, about my friend Lin. I asked you could she come to stay and you never said yes or no. I just wondered, were you by any chance planning a surprise? Were you going to say we can pay for her air ticket? Because if we can do that, then it should be now.' He could hear his brothers demanding in the background: 'Ask him has it snowed yet!'

'About Lin, can she come? Can we pay her ticket, this Christmas? I know it's short notice but it's important. I can't explain in detail, but it would be a really good deed.'

'You mean your friend Lin O'Falloren?'

'Yes, O'Falloren. Just like your's and Daddy's friend, I told you. But I don't think there can be any connection because she's never been to Africa, though I suppose she might be a distant relation. Can she come? Please?'

'Lin O'Falloren. Hmm . . .' He could imagine his mother's face, her lips pursed: her long, tapered fingers tapping on the phone handset. 'That's funny.'

'What's funny? Why is it funny?'

His brothers and his little sister were still yelling, 'Ask him if he's seen any snow!' Opie repeating it patiently, the way little children will go on and on until their question is answered; Okiye and Dominic chanting the question to be annoying, typical brats. The line was so clear it was as if he was in that room in Africa, but somehow blinded and wrapped in a cold mist.

'Maybe I'll get your daddy to ring Breadford,' said his mother at last. 'Listen, Oya, don't tell your friend you spoke to us, not until she talks to you. Don't say anything, until I find out what's happened about something. Be careful about that, we don't want to raise false hopes.'

'So can she come for Christmas?' he persisted, trying to get a straight answer.

'Maybe another time, sweetheart, maybe another time.'

They talked some more, about Oya's travel arrangements, and he hung up feeling deeply disappointed. It would have been such a good solution. He wished he was going home tomorrow. He didn't want his mother's disembodied voice. He wanted her every day, coming in from her work to find him having his afternoon snack on the verandah; or there when he came home from school, talking about ordinary things. But he didn't want to leave Lin alone. It was strange the way his mother had said, *Don't tell.* That was exactly what Lin had kept saying, when she behaved so crazily in the Museum. It seemed to Oya that his friend was surrounded by secrets and invisible obstacles. It was like a conspiracy. He could almost believe that she was right. There was some mysterious, malign power at work.

Mr Vernon popped his head round the door. 'Finished? I hope everybody's well.'

'Yes, thanks.'

He came in and started excavating in the mounds of paper. 'Now where did I put those carol sheets? I rely on you to be at the rehearsal this evening. I'm expecting the Madison girls: your friend Lin, and Nathalie and Megan and their mother. I hope they all turn up. We need new blood!'

Outside the study's tall windows a few flakes of snow

were drifting in the darkness. Oya shivered. It might sound romantic if you were in Africa, but he hated the snow. It was like the ghost of honest life-giving rain: blank and sinister, falling without a sound, filling the air with sly white prickles. I'll see her at the carol rehearsal, he consoled himself. I'll be able to make sure she's all right. But he was sure she *wasn't* all right. Something was happening to Lin, something terrible was approaching. He could feel it in the cold breath of the snow.

Village carol singing was exactly the sort of activity that had featured in Auntie Sylvia's dreams of rural living. But now that the winter had really begun she was torn between her greedy desire for the country life – those up-market traditional gatherings, the old-fashioned parties where her girls would meet the nicest sort of people – and her hatred of the mess and effort caused by bad weather. She wanted to have a huge tree, she wanted Uncle Derek to take the children out into the woods to gather boughs of holly. She was planning to have all the Carol Singers round for mulled wine and mince pies. But the thought of driving a half mile along a Devon lane in actual snowfall horrified her.

'You're the one who wanted to live in the country, Mum,' jeered Megan.

'They're not going to grit our approach. I phoned the county council. It seems we'd have to pay some outrageous amount. That's disgusting. Imagine if we got stuck in the snow. Out on that moor, you wouldn't survive an hour.'

'Yeah, terrifying,' drawled Nathalie. 'But there isn't any moor between here and the village. What do you want to do? Ring a taxi which won't turn up? Or get the bus that doesn't exist?'

Elinor was staying behind to babysit, because Uncle Derek was still in town and wouldn't be home until late. She suggested they should walk, and earned a slap for coming out with such a cheeky idea. Nathalie and Megan had a spat about a knitted hat that Megan had taken from Nathalie's drawer. Auntie Sylvia changed her shoes three times, from smart to practical and back again. At last Elinor saw the three of them out of the house. She watched from the scullery porch until the Espace had crept on to the lane, headlights blazing, through darkness speckled with a few vagrant dots of white. Then she had a tussle with Dekkie, who was convinced that ten snowflakes justified taking his toboggan out into the garden *right now.*

'Come on, Dekkie,' she coaxed. 'I'll run you a big bath with bubbles. We'll play blowing foam at each other, the way we used to when you were little.'

'Don't call me that!' he roared. 'Don't call me that baby name. You're not my sister! You're no one. You can't tell me what to do. *Pig's breath, can't dance, Elinor's got dirty pants!*'

This was Megan's latest anti-Elinor chant. Nathalie had relaxed some of her bullying since Elinor had made friends with Oya. But Megan and Derek had eagerly taken over. She finally managed to get Derek to bed, and settled in front of the television. She felt a bit like Cinderella, but she was used to that role. She didn't mind missing the carol practice. Auntie Sylvia would be nervous, so she'd get angry with Megan and Nathalie over something. Then she'd take it out on Elinor, and embarrass everyone. It was much better to be left behind.

She didn't know why she had such a strange feeling that *they shouldn't have left her alone.*

She was trying not to think about what had happened on Saturday. She hoped she'd managed to convince Oya that there was nothing much wrong. She did not remember anything about it herself. They had been in the Museum – a horrible place, full of rotten old things. She'd picked up a leaflet, for something to do. The next thing she knew she had been on the floor with Oya's face peering at her anxiously. She must have fainted. But she wouldn't think about it. She wouldn't think about Dekkie either, though he'd hurt her feelings. It was silly to be upset. She would concentrate on the rare luxury of an evening to herself in the cosy front room, instead of being trapped in her torture chamber of a bedroom. There was a book in her hand but she wasn't reading. Voices from the TV faded to a soothing blur . . .

She could hear a child crying. The sound wasn't loud, but it was getting on her nerves. She wondered why no one else could hear it. People came and searched the house from top to bottom, but there wasn't any child there. Sometimes she couldn't hear the sound herself. Loud voices called in the yard, hooves and boots tramped, wheels came rumbling. There were anxious and heated discussions muffled behind closed doors. She hoped the crying had stopped, but at night it came back. If she held her breath she could almost make out pleading words. When she fell asleep in her truckle bed, worn out by that hateful sound, she dreamed that she held Diccon in her arms. 'Ssh' she murmured, stroking his soft hair back from his dear face, the way she'd soothed him when she'd come to be his nursemaid; when she'd first lost her own mother. He mustn't cry because Aunt Deborah would be angry. 'Shssh, my dear love, my lambkin, my comfort. Don't you fret, Nelly's here.' She woke, and her arms were empty. She could still feel the warmth of the child's body. It filled her with terror.

Far off and half drowned in the wind, she could hear that crying.

Sleeping, Elinor struggled to escape from the dream. She fought with all her strength and with a great effort she managed to wake; or seemed to wake. She was in the back of the Espace. The big car bowled along silently. She and

Dekkie were in the rear seats. In front of her she saw Nathalie and Megan's heads and shoulders, and then the heads and shoulders of her aunt and uncle. They were like cut-outs made of cardboard. Hot sunlight poured through the windows. They were sightseeing on Dartmoor. Elinor was carsick and miserable. Dekkie was being naughty. He was dropping things out of his window. She knew she'd be blamed when Auntie Sylvia found out about the trail they were leaving behind them. But she couldn't make him stop. He grinned and pulled gargoyle faces. When she managed to speak her voice was a tiny hoarse whisper: *stop it.* Dekkie just laughed. He was grimacing so that he scarcely looked human. She remembered that she used to love him once, but that feeling seemed far, far away. He was the son of the family, he had everything. Why should she pity him?

If only that noise would stop, stop, stop . . .

'Stop it, Dekkie,' she whispered. 'Stop crying, stop it now or I'll –'

But he started crying more loudly, roaring and beating at her with his fists. 'Don't call me that!' he yelled. 'Don't call me that baby name! You're not my sister, you're no one!' They weren't in the back of the Espace any more. She didn't know quite where she was, but Dekkie was making such an awful noise. She was going to have to shut him up.

I'll make him quiet.

Suddenly, a car door slammed.

Elinor started to wake.

Where was she? To her bewilderment she wasn't curled up on the sofa in the big front room. She was standing in the passageway, upstairs. She was outside the door of Dekkie's bedroom, in her stockinged feet. There was something in her hands. It wasn't the book she'd been holding when she fell asleep. It was one of the scatter cushions from the sofa, a plump pillow covered in violet raw silk and trimmed with primrose cord.

There was not a sound from the little boy's room.

'Thank goodness the snow held off,' came her aunt's voice.

More doors opened and slammed. 'Where's Elinor?' demanded Megan loudly.

'She must have gone to bed.'

'She's let the fire go out, the lazy pig.'

'I hope she *hasn't* gone to bed!' snapped Aunt Sylvia. 'I told her to stay up. What if your father had rung? What if Dekkie needed anything?'

Elinor hid the scatter cushion in the airing cupboard, and went down to face the family.

'I was checking that Dekkie was all right,' she explained. 'I thought I heard him crying.'

'And is he?'

'What?'

'*Is he all right?*' repeated Auntie Sylvia, with sarcastic patience.

'I d-don't know,' faltered Elinor.

Nathalie and Megan and Aunt Sylvia's faces were all turned to her, as she stood in the doorway to the kitchen stairs. Their eyes were bright, their cheeks rosy from the cold. They looked so smug. Something was twisting inside her, like a knife in her mind. She knew of a way to wipe those bright, hard smiles away. After all these months, she suddenly really understood what the haunting meant. She could make the Madisons sorry, that was what the ghosts were trying to tell her. She could make it so they wished they were like poor Nelly and had no family. She could make them wish they'd never been born.

'What on earth's the matter with the girl?' demanded Aunt Sylvia, of no one in particular. 'She looks as if she's been walking in her sleep.'

'Planet Earth to Elinor!' yodelled Megan. 'Elinor's going mental!'

Then a car drove up outside with a crunch and a roar. Uncle Derek was home. His wife and daughters were distracted from their prey, and Elinor managed to get away without any more questioning. She slept better than usual that night. She even felt a strange kind of relief, when she found herself alone in the panelled room. But next morning when she woke that mood had gone, and she felt a new kind of dread.

Dekkie was in the front room when she went through to the scullery, as usual, to wash and brush her teeth in the little cloakroom. He was watching TV in his pyjamas. His eyes followed her slyly as she passed. She heard him singing under his breath: *Pig's breath, can't dance, Elinor's got dirty pants.* How fat and pink his cheeks were. When he grinned his eyes were mean slits. He looked exactly like a pig, like the pig-baby in *Alice.* Someone ought to smother him, she thought. Squash his fat face flat, it would be an improvement. Of course she didn't mean that, not seriously. Yet for a mad moment she thought she ought to warn someone, in case Dekkie was in genuine danger. But even to Elinor herself the words she might have spoken sounded ridiculous, outlandish, unbelievable. She couldn't tell.

Oya had his air ticket. He was leaving on Monday December 22nd, going home for three weeks. He wasn't, to his disappointment, travelling alone. He'd be joining some friends of his mother's at Heathrow. He was excited, but anxious for Lin. Nothing else *bad* had happened since that Saturday in Eaxby. He hadn't spotted the stalker again, and she hadn't started babbling about gruesome local history. But he saw her trying to do her homework on the bus, and she wasn't the type to do that unless things were getting out of control. He knew from the look of her swollen, weary eyes that she wasn't sleeping. It was like watching his most trusted companion, on the hard trek of his expedition, growing weaker by the day. If she didn't reach a cache of food and a shelter soon, she wasn't going to make it.

One evening when he was at the Rectory doing his homework, he broke down and asked Mr Vernon, trying to be discreet. 'Mr Vernon, suppose you had a friend who seemed to be in real trouble, and she, the friend I mean, made you promise not to tell, what would you do?'

The vicar took off his glasses and fidgeted with the mended bit, which had once been fixed with tape but was now held together by a twist of wire. This was something he did when he was trying to concentrate his mind. 'Hmm. Is this an actual case?' he asked.

'It's Lin. I'm worried about Lin Madison,' confessed Oya. 'She asked me not to tell anyone, but someone's been following her around. She's not imagining it, because I saw her stalker too! She's very frightened. But you know what the Madisons are like with Lin. She won't tell them, I think it's because she's sure they'd be no help. She's got no one else, and it's getting her down. She's scared of her own shadow.'

Mr Vernon peered at Oya shortsightedly. 'Lin Madison. Ah. I thought it might be. Oh dear.' He put his glasses back on. 'Scared of her shadow,' he repeated. 'I see . . . Well, thank you for telling me, Oya. You can leave it with me. I've been meaning to do something about Lin's situation. I must definitely do something. I have it on my list –' The next moment something on the heaped table caught his eye. He dived for a piece of paper among the thousands. 'Ah, *there* it is! Family Christmas Dinners for Those Lonely at Christmas. I've been searching everywhere for this document. I must sort the Lonely out at once.' And he hurried away, calling for Mrs Manaton.

Lin was worse than alone, but she wasn't on the top of anybody's *to do* list: and she was avoiding Oya. Sometimes when they met in school she looked right through him, as if he wasn't there.

Elinor was not consciously avoiding Oya. She didn't notice that she was making him more and more anxious. She was fighting a lonely battle, and could think of nothing else. No one knew it, but she had not slept in the fourposter bed since that morning in November when she had woken to find the imprint of a child's body beside her. For a while after that day she had helplessly gone through the motions of getting ready, and climbing into the hateful canopied prison. Each night, after an hour or so of open-eyed misery, terror had finally given her the strength to escape. She had slipped down, dragged her duvet over to the rug by the fireplace and tried to sleep there instead. In the mornings, so that Auntie Sylvia wouldn't find out what she was doing, she would spread the quilt quickly in place, averting her eyes so she didn't see whether there was any sign of strange disturbance in the sheets.

Since the time she'd found herself outside Dekkie's bedroom with a cushion in her hands, she had been trying not to fall asleep at all. She did not ask herself exactly why she must stay awake. She avoided thoughts that led to the edge of the abyss. But she would wash and change into her pyjamas, and then sit up in a chair with her duvet wrapped around her. Sometimes she kept her desklamp on, braving the risk that Auntie Sylvia would come down to the front hall for some reason and spot the light. It made no difference. She hardly had to close her eyes now, before the dreams came. Scenes and voices crowded into her weary mind, as she dozed and struggled on the edge of sleep. She was back in that cold spring of long ago, and the interrupted story was taken up again . . .

Nelly scrubbed the floors. She cleaned the candlesticks,

she made the fires. She scraped pans and polished knives and carried water. For the housework must be done, though the household was plunged into grief and confusion. The drunken cook had been sent away. Other servants had come to tend their distraught mistress, who refused to leave the Dower House as long as there was any hope. They barely spoke to poor Nelly. She had never made friends at the big house. The maids had been envious of her, the older staff had resented her position as Diccon's companion. Now she paid the price. No one spoke a word of comfort to Mistress Deborah's poor relation, who had become a mere scullery maid. No one shared the rough work. There were more exciting things to do, at this tragic time.

Strangers came and left, filling the Dower House with a cruel mockery of bustle and life. The master came home, a stricken man. It was many days, Nelly had lost count of them, since Diccon had vanished: but the search, which had been abandoned, was begun over again. The servants whispered. They spoke of something which Nelly had guessed, that night when she saw her Aunt Deborah wearing a man's riding clothes. Mistress Deborah was with child again. It was feared that she would lose this baby too, because she was half out of her wits with grief.

'Poor Mistress, you should have seen her face, when they brought in the child's boots and crop from the stable. White as a mushroom, and those great eyes of hers, staring –'

'It's a wicked shame. Bad enough to lose the child to the moor, but it begins to look as if there's worse to be known . . .'

The doctor prescribed strong sleeping powders and ordered that the lady should not be left alone, night or day. For Nelly the only prescription was her work. She tried to hide herself in the never-ending chores, but she knew that the whispers were turning against her. She felt the eyes that fell on her bent back as she scrubbed and swept and cleaned. They wanted a scapegoat, so they picked on Nelly: the stranger, the poor friendless maid.

They asked questions.

'Why did you hide Master Diccon's crop and boots and hat in the stable?'

She said, 'I didn't know.'

They asked, 'How can you have hidden these articles without knowing why you did so?'

She said, 'I did not understand you, Sirs. I should have said, I did not know the articles were hidden.'

They asked, 'Did you steal a pair of amber earrings?'

She said she did not.

'What can you tell us about Master Diccon's disappearance? Speak the truth.'

'I didn't do it,' she told them. 'I swear to God I did not harm him.'

The big men in their big wigs, in their broadcloth coats with the shining brass buttons, looked on poor Nelly with horror in their great grave faces. She thought of the trouble of polishing those buttons. They told her to go. They did not ask her the question that she must not answer.

Did you ever hear a child crying?

No one went near the panelled room. It had been searched with the rest of the house and outbuildings when Diccon first went missing. But there was no reason now why anyone would go to that dark little study at the end of the blind passage off the front hall. Only the maid of all work, who had to keep the house clean and swept: and even she didn't go into that room. It was locked and she was glad. She would not like to go in there, night or day.

Elinor was never really sleeping. But she would wake or recover from these dreams that were half waking nightmares, and see the panelled room again as it was in her own time. Then, after a moment or two, she would begin to hear the sound of a child crying. First a whimper, then a cough; and then the low, endless, patient sobbing. It was almost worse when, as sometimes happened, she could hear nothing. *Because she knew it hadn't gone away.* If only she could make it stop!

She knew there was only one way to do that.

She would not let herself think about it, but she knew the price of freedom.

Once, when she was sitting there awake, she heard something stirring. She had her lamp beside her chair, but it wasn't switched on. It was another kind of light that showed her the fourposter bed; a faint glow that came from nowhere. She was facing the end of the bed, and the curtains were pulled back. She clearly saw a body that moved restlessly, like someone tossing and turning in a nightmare. Suddenly the figure sat bolt upright. It was the hideous old woman she had seen once before, searching the drawers of the walnut desk. The white face stared ahead, with eyes as black as pitch. Then the woman got out of bed, moving with a horrible, jerky agility. She was wearing a brocade gown, the same as she'd been wearing the first time. It hung on her scrawny old body. Quickly she crossed the room, her rich skirts flickering as if dipped in flame. She looked round once, fixing Elinor with those terrible eyes: and then, in the corner by the passage door, she disappeared.

Elinor was sure now that it was no use trying to get rid of the yellow ear-bobs. She knew that whatever she tried, somehow she would be prevented. The estate agents would be shut again, or they would say *we can't trace the owners, so the earrings belong to you.* There was no escape by that route. She thought about telling Oya the whole story. But that was no use either. He was brave and loyal, but *he was a child.* She felt a hundred years older than him. She'd never be able to make him understand.

The worst part was that she could not trust herself. The real Elinor, the person she wanted to be, hated those earrings and longed to get rid of them. But there was another Elinor, who still coveted the yellow ear-bobs. She'd taken them when she knew it was stealing, and when she had clearly sensed that they were evil. She still wanted them now. The real Elinor would have been in no danger of letting the ghosts make her do something horrible. The real Elinor was Lin O'Falloren, the brave, clever girl who was going to grow up and get away and live her own life. Unfortunately she wasn't in charge. It was Elinor the miserable, bullied poor relation who was in control. You couldn't rely on Elinor. She was too cowed and battered to be trusted. She wanted to get her own back on the Madisons, and she didn't have the power to resist evil. Elinor was weak, and that made her very, very dangerous. And then there was Nelly, poor Nelly. She wasn't wicked, and she wasn't really stupid: but she was a child whose mind had never had a chance to grow. She didn't know the difference between right and wrong. If you could reach Nelly, if you could explain to her, you could stop the terrible thing happening. But that couldn't be, it was too late, the past was fixed . . .

One morning in the second week of December Elinor found herself in the library at school, writing about the different Elinors when she was supposed to be revising her notes for a history test. She'd decided to try and set down what she thought was happening, to see if it would clear her mind. When she read what she had written, she felt very scared indeed. She scrumpled up the sheet, tore it into pieces and stuffed the pieces into her school bag. She was so frightened by what was revealed there that she didn't dare to dump the scraps in a school wastepaper bin. If she was really thinking like this, as if there were three Elinors in her head, then *she was going crazy.* It was as if she was falling down a cliff. She had started falling that morning when she woke and found that she'd been sleeping with a ghost child in her arms. She'd been able to cling to bushes and scrabble at footholds, but there was nothing left now between her and the sheer drop. She must pull herself back: but how? She felt the depths calling to her, dragging at her, as if she was being pulled into blackness by an immense weight . . . Oya was right. *She had to talk to someone*, someone grown-up. She would talk to Mr Vernon. In the end, much as she dreaded that conversation, she thought she could trust him. But no one else must know, not even Oya himself. The things that she would have to say were too horrible.

Mr Vernon was even more tremendously busy than usual, because of Christmas. There was no chance that she'd be able to drop in for a quiet chat at the Rectory. They'd be interrupted ten times a minute, and she didn't fancy that. But no matter how busy he was, she knew he made a point of being in his office at the church between six and seven on a Wednesday evening. That was where people went if they had something private to discuss. It would not be easy for Elinor to get there, because six to seven was cooking time at the Dower House and Auntie Sylvia expected her to be in the kitchen. But she thought she could manage it. Desperation made her cunning.

On the second Wednesday in December, after school, Auntie Sylvia wanted her to make a vegetable soup, a *proper* soup, not something out of a packet. Elinor pared and chopped the vegetables swiftly. She'd never liked cooking much. She'd wondered bitterly why it was never Nathalie or Megan's turn to have to rush their homework after all the chores were done. She used to promise herself that when she was grown up she'd live on chips and chocolate bars for the rest of her life. Now she hated the work. It brought the shadows closer, it made her feel that

Nelly the poor servant girl was taking over. Her hands became Nelly's hands, her shoulders stooped and ached like Nelly's. But she fought off the nightmare. When it was time to leave, in order to get to Breadford to see Mr Vernon, she went to find Aunt Sylvia and reported that there was no salt. Her aunt came and banged about in the cupboards, tried three different salt shakers, slapped Elinor, and was finally convinced.

'How could that happen! I don't know *what* you've done with it, you little pest, but you'll have to go and fetch some more. You can get me another jar of deluxe mincemeat while you're at it, if that nasty little store has anything like that. And if I find that salt in the meantime, there will be trouble, young lady.' She was baking her own mince pies, much to the disgust of her husband and children, who preferred the supermarket kind.

Elinor didn't think the missing salt would be found. She had slipped out of the back door and poured it over the fence into the marshy field where the bullocks lived: where it had instantly vanished into a pool of mud.

As she pedalled slowly up the lane the front light on her bike made a glowing, moving cone of visible night. Once a pair of green eyes suddenly stared at her from near the ground. Maybe it was a fox, or just a cat. The cold air pumped life into her veins. This darkness was so different from the dark in the panelled room. She wished she could go on cycling forever. It would be so peaceful. She remembered what Auntie Sylvia had said the night it had almost snowed. *Out on that moor, you wouldn't last an hour.* She could lose herself up there, where the searchers had found no trace of Richard Revelle. She could ride out and never come back, the way they said Diccon had done. That would be some kind of solution. But then the lights of Breadford shone in front of her, and she was back in present reality.

She went to the supermarket first. She bought a pack of salt; and the nearest she could find to 'deluxe mincemeat'. 'Put your own brandy in it, my dear,' said the lady at the till. 'That's what we do at our house. Making your own isn't worth the trouble or the money, but a drop of cheap brandy do cheer up the shop-bought stuff no end. You tell your mum.'

She stuffed the jar and the packet in her bike bag and headed for the church.

There were lights in the tall windows at the front of the Rectory. That was Mr Vernon's study. The curtains were open. She could see Oya doing his homework. She could see the top of his bent head, over the piles of Mr Vernon's papers. She stopped pedalling, to stand for a moment watching. How far away he looked. If she could only wrench herself out of this terrible state of mind and get back to normal unhappiness. The problems that she used to have seemed so trivial when she looked back at them. She saw herself, strengthened and calm after whatever Mr Vernon said to her, going back to the Dower House and standing up to Auntie Sylvia. *I simply can't stick it in that room with the fourposter*, she would say. *I think it's haunted. I don't care if you believe me or not, so long as you don't make me stay in there another night. I want you to buy me a new bed and I want to move into one of the empty bedrooms. I don't mind about the damp, I want to do it now.* Then her nightmare imaginings would vanish into nothing. There'd be no more watcher in the shadows. The amber earrings would be nothing but a pair of earrings. She wouldn't be afraid she was going mad.

She pushed her bike up the path to the churchyard, and locked it by the gate. Not that anyone was going to come along and steal it, but it was reassuring to take her usual precautions. She slung the bike bag over her shoulder, for the same reason: and felt like an intrepid explorer, like one of Oya's heroes setting out to do something daring. Salt and mincemeat weren't very sensible supplies but they would have to do.

She wondered what did other people talk about when they came to have a private chat with the vicar? In the olden days, it would have been called *confession*. Mr Vernon was sitting there waiting for people to come and tell him their sins. Then he'd pray with them for God's help to make things right. It was comforting to think that others had done the same as her, though probably not many of them had had such a bizarre story to tell. Thousands of people had walked up this path with their hearts in their mouths, and a need to share some secret burden.

She was close to the church before she heard the voices. One of them was Mr Vernon's. The other was a woman's voice, low and strangely accented. Light reached out into the darkness to gleam on the mellow stonework of the north porch, the gravel of the path; the green mesh of the bin for old funeral flowers. Mr Vernon and his last visitor were coming out. Elinor didn't want to invade someone else's privacy; and she didn't want to be seen. She stepped off the path and ducked behind a gravestone. When she peered around it she saw Mr Vernon in the porch. The person he was talking to stood against the light, like a figure cut out of black paper: someone in a hat with a brim and a long full-skirted coat. She heard that voice again, low, strong, and filled with unmistakable menace. She crouched back, trembling. *Surely she knew that voice*? Mr Vernon went back inside and shut the door to his office, which was a little room off the vestry. The other speaker came into view, walking quickly down the path. In the sudden darkness Elinor could dimly make out a gleam of fair curls under the hat brim: a caped, dark coat, a gloved hand . . .

Her heart started to pound like a road drill. She fell against the gravestone, clutching her bike bag in her arms. At last, hardly knowing what she was doing, she stumbled back to the gate, unlocked her bike with shaking fingers and fled.

By the time she'd cycled back to the Dower House, handed over the shopping and the change, and been yelled at and slapped for taking so long, Elinor knew she couldn't have seen the vicar of Breadford talking to a ghost. That couldn't be true. Either she'd imagined the whole thing, or she had mistaken some innocent parishioner for the watcher who dogged her footsteps and haunted her waking dreams. I'll try again, she told herself. I'll try again next week. But she knew she wouldn't do it. Her last chance of rescue was gone.

Nine

THEY DID NOT TAKE NELLY FROM THE DOWER House. They came for her when the Dower House was shut up, and the whole household had removed back to Revelle Manor. The rebuilding work had turned everything to chaos. Nelly had been distressed to find that the room which she had once shared with Diccon was no more. She had cried a great deal, at night, in the loft over the dairy where she'd been allotted a bed among the other young maidservants. This was held against her. They said an innocent maid would not have threshed and cried like that, or woken shrieking from her sleep. They took her into Eaxby and placed her in the Bridewell – the odd little tower of stone by the market cross, cold as a well, where they kept criminals.

They'd put her by herself in a room that contained nothing but a straw-filled mattress that was crawling with vermin, and a dirty blanket. It was not decent, they said, to put her in the common room with the town drunkards and the like. She was the only maid they had in the Bridewell, and the youngest prisoner it had ever known. She heard the men who came to take her for her daily questioning laughing and muttering outside her door. It must be morning: she could not tell. The only window was tightly shuttered. She would have to ask if she might relieve herself. She had held her water, for however long she had been locked in, because she could not bring herself to piddle in the room where she slept, like a beast. She had been brought up differently from that. She was afraid of having to stay here until her monthlies came. How could she speak to men about something like that? So far, humiliation and the dark were her worst fears. That, and the crying. When the wind was in the wrong quarter she could still hear it, though she stopped her ears.

They should not keep her shut up alone like this, so young. But she was a friendless maid and the magistrate was Simon Revelle, who had no reason to see that she was treated gently. They should not question her so hard. They kept on and on, determined that she would break down and confess her guilt. But they could not find the yellow ear-bobs. She clung to that thought, and thanked God. As long as they could not find the ear-bobs, they could not prove she had stolen them, and poor Nelly's life would be safe. The laughing and banging grew louder. Suddenly the door of her prison burst open. In shock and fright she lost control of herself. She felt a rush of warm liquid, and woke in fear and shame.

'What are you doing sleeping on the floor?' demanded Megan.

'Get up, lazybones!' cried Nathalie. 'We're going Christmas shopping with Dad. And you'd better buy me something decent, skinflint, or you'll be sorry.'

Elinor's cousins, who had burst into the room together, stood looking down at her. Derek was with his sisters. It was Saturday again. Christmas coming soon. Nathalie marched over to the windows and flung back Elinor's shabby curtains. Winter sunshine flooded in. Elinor cowered, still half caught up in the dream.

'What's that smell?' asked Derek loudly, with a big mean grin.

He knew perfectly well what the smell was. He wet the bed often enough himself. Elinor knew that. She was the one who stripped the sheets and stuffed them in the machine before leaving for school.

'Oh no, *she's wet the bed!*' groaned Megan, imitating her big sister's drawl. 'Is *that* why you're sleeping on the floor? How disgusting!' She hauled the quilt away. Derek ran out into the front hall, eager to tell his mother the news.

'Mum! Mum! Elinor's wet the bed! She's wetted all her duvet!'

Auntie Sylvia was furious. She forced Elinor to wash the stained cover and her nightclothes by hand. 'At your age!' she stormed. 'How could you do this to me?' As a punishment, she was not allowed to come shopping. The Madisons rushed about, collecting their outdoor things and loudly complaining that Elinor had made everyone late. Elinor's hot tears fell into the soapy water while her aunt stood over her, hectoring. 'Really, Elinor, I don't know what we're going to do with you. You've never, never tried to be one of the family. I ask you to do the least thing and you look at me with that smartypants cold face on you. Don't think I don't notice your insolence. And now this. What are you? Some kind of animal?'

'Please don't. Please, Aunt Sylvia, don't –'

'You act so meek but you've got a hard, hard little heart. I know you. You may fool your friends at the Rectory and your little African prince. Don't think you can fool me!'

At last they drove away. Elinor hung the duvet cover and her pyjamas out in the yard. The day was cold and bright. A great tit was singing in the trees that edged the lawn: *chee-chaw, chee-chaw, chee-chaw!* Nothing had been done to the garden since they moved in. Auntie Sylvia had grand plans, but they were waiting until the house was fixed. The vegetable rows lay fallow and weed-grown. '*She doesn't mean it,*' she whispered. She believed this was true. Auntie Sylvia didn't have any plan to hurt Elinor. She had a bad temper and an uncontrolled tongue, and a need to lash out. Whenever she was particularly nasty to Elinor, you could bet Uncle Derek had been working late again, or else Nathalie had been nasty to her mother first. Saying things like, '*Don't wear that make-up, it's too young for you,*' or '*You look awful in that dress. No wonder Dad doesn't fancy you any more.*' Nathalie was full of gems like that.

Had her life with the Madisons always been so bad? Had they always been such an unhappy family? Or was it this house? Maybe the ghosts of the Dower House were making life worse for everyone, and Elinor suffered more because she was at the bottom of the heap. She looked with longing at the slope of moorland that reached up to the pale, glittering sky, beyond the garden fence and beyond the bullocks' field. Freedom was like that skyline: so near and so far away. She felt as if she could reach out and touch it. She could change everything with one single, simple effort. But the moor was full of sinking holes and hidden mineshafts. You could get lost up there. You could die.

She had been sitting still for too long. She could hear the crying again. In the daytime it was thin and faint. She could stop herself from noticing it as long as she was busy. But if everything was quiet, if she had nothing to do and no one was talking to her, it grew until it filled her mind. 'Stop it!' wailed Elinor, clutching her head in her hands. 'Stop it! Stop it!'

The day passed. There were blank spaces in it. She couldn't bring herself to leave the house and garden, so she did chores to keep herself occupied. She scrubbed the kitchen floor. She polished the knives and forks, and dusted the little places that don't often get dusted in a modern house, a house without servants. She must work to quiet that faint sound of sobbing: 'What is it you want?' she cried. 'Just *tell me!* I'll do anything –'

There was no answer. There was no need for the ghosts to answer. She knew.

The Madisons came back long after dark, happily full of restaurant lunch and tea and Christmas spirit. They laughed at Elinor because she'd hung out her washing and forgotten to bring it in. The frost had settled as soon as the sun went down, and everything was stiff as a board. But they weren't angry. They'd forgotten completely how mean they'd all been to her in the morning. Uncle Derek was in such a good mood he offered to take Auntie Sylvia out to the White Hart, the pub she preferred in Breadford, of his own free will.

'Come here,' said Auntie Sylvia with a secretive smile, while the cousins rushed upstairs to hide their purchases. She led Elinor into the study. 'Don't look so timid, you silly girl. I'm only going to show you what I bought for you to give to your cousins.' She lifted packages out of a carrier bag and displayed them. 'This game is for Derek. The nice make-up case is for Nathalie, I know she's wanting a new one, and the scarf and gloves are for Megan. They'll suit her, don't you think? Really elegant, they'll make her feel so grown-up. So that's them settled. I'll give you some money to go out and spend on me and your uncle another day. All forgotten and forgiven, then?' She watched Elinor's face, her indulgent smile fading. 'What's the matter? Aren't you satisfied?'

'I-I don't have that kind of money,' said Elinor, staring at the expensive presents.

'Yes you do, dear. It's coming out of your building society, so that's all right.'

Elinor's building society account was where her uncle and aunt saved up her child benefit payments. As Auntie Sylvia had often told her, it was very good of them to do this because they weren't made of money. One day when she was older she'd need those savings and more if she wanted to go to college. They couldn't support her forever, not with three children of their own to think of. The building society account was sacred. It couldn't be touched, not for any reason. Elinor had never even been threatened with any loss of that money.

But she simply nodded. Life was like that, she thought. Any time you'd made up your mind to be strong and bear things bravely, another blow came and whacked you down, from the only direction you hadn't expected. But she had fooled life this time, because she really didn't care. She didn't care about anything, if only that horrible crying would stop.

'Yes, Auntie Sylvia. That's fine.'

She went to bed before the others, and long before Auntie Sylvia and Uncle Derek came back from the pub. Derek was watching TV with his sisters. He ought to be in bed, but they were feeling Christmassy so they were letting him stay up. They told Elinor that *she* could try to make Dekkie go to bed if she felt like it, since she was the official babysitter. This was a joke. They were in a good mood, and could hardly be bothered to tease. But it was a luxury to leave them: a treat that she allowed herself because she *didn't care.*

The panelled room was cold, so cold. The rug was still damp from where she'd scrubbed the stain she'd made when she'd wet herself in her sleep. She fetched a blanket from the airing cupboard to cover the patch, and a spare duvet. She put on a heavy jumper over her pyjamas. Then, moved by an impulse that she could not control, she groped for the catch under the cabinet door of the walnut desk, and took the amber earrings from their hiding place. She had not looked at them for days. She didn't have to look at them. Their presence was as constant in her mind as the sound of the crying child. The amber glowed against her palm, but the silver had begun to tarnish again. 'I'm going to take you,' she whispered. 'I'm going to take you up on the moor and drop you down a mineshaft, you wicked things.'

The yellow ear-bobs knew it was an idle threat.

She fell asleep in spite of the cold, with the earrings clutched in her hand.

She slept, and dreamed. It was a different kind of dream this time. She seemed to wake, still in the panelled room. A tiny fire burned in the grate, and there were two candles burning. But the room felt damp and cold, and there was a smell of stale neglect. An upright figure with high piled hair sat at the window with its back to Elinor. The figure looked young until it slowly turned, and stared at her with the eyes of a damned soul.

She screamed and woke, sitting upright, rigid with terror. She thought her screaming must have woken the whole house. But nothing stirred. She lay down again and fell into an uneasy doze, where Dekkie was crawling after her down a long, dark tunnel. She was trying to get away, to save herself from being buried alive, but he howled and grabbed on to her clothes. She couldn't shake him off, and his crying went through her like the sound of nails on a blackboard. Then she woke again, and at last everything was simple. Everything else was a dream but this: *she had to do what the ghosts wanted.* She didn't know why she'd ever hesitated. She must be free of this torment. She must be free.

The full moon blazed in at her window. She got up and went quietly through the sleeping house. Derek's toys were scattered on the carpet in front of the TV, but she picked her way through those booby traps with ease, without making a sound. She didn't switch on a light until she was in the kitchen. The kitchen gleamed. Everything was painfully bright and clean, because Nelly had spent the whole day there, slaving at her chores. She knew her aunt was going to be pleased, especially because the crying would have stopped. She had been wrong to think of what she was going to do as a wicked revenge against the family that had spurned her. It wasn't revenge, it was *necessary*. Elinor had to become Nelly, and do what they said Nelly had done: so that at last she could rest.

The ordinary kitchen knives were kept on a magnetic strip against the wall. The best knives, the expensive ones, were housed in a solid block of varnished pine, each one buried to the neck in its own special slot. She selected one of these carefully, and drew it out. It had a tapering twelve-inch blade, a long narrow vicious triangle of acid-bright metal. She knew that the edge was very, very sharp. She knew she would be able to use it. She would not falter. Softly up the stairs, and into the little boy's room. In a few minutes it would be over.

'*Elinor*?'

She heard her aunt's voice. She saw her aunt standing in front of her in the over-bright room, in a fancy silk kimono, feet encased in the cosy puppy-dog slippers that better reflected her real taste. But Elinor thought she was dreaming. She laughed, because Aunt Sylvia wasn't really there and the knife was still in her hand.

'For heaven's sake. I think the child's sleepwalking! *Elinor, put that knife down!*'

She woke up. She found herself standing in the kitchen, the same as she had been in her dream. She was standing in the kitchen, a razor-sharp butcher's knife in her hand, staring at Auntie Sylvia, who was staring back with something in her face that was almost like fear.

'He was crying,' said Elinor, and heard her own voice dimly, like a buzzing in her head. 'He kept on and on. No one could hear it but me. He wouldn't stop. So I had to stop him.'

'What on earth are you talking about? Put that thing down!'

Then she was really awake. The knife dropped from her hand. She began to laugh, in sheer panic and horror. If Auntie Sylvia knew! If she had any idea what Elinor had meant to do! She had been going to kill her cousin Dekkie. It had seemed so real. *It had been real.* It could have happened! She laughed and laughed and couldn't stop.

'Oh, for heaven's sake,' exclaimed her aunt, habit overcoming her astonishment. She lifted her hand in an all too familiar gesture.

Elinor took a step backwards. 'I'm too old to be slapped,' she said.

For the first time in her life.

Slowly Auntie Sylvia lowered her hand. She picked up the knife and replaced it in the block. 'You were sleep-walking,' she said. 'Are you awake now? Are you feeling all right?'

'Yes. I'm fine.'

'Maybe I'd better make you a warm drink,' suggested Auntie Sylvia, almost timidly.

'No, thank you.'

'Well, if you're sure –'

'I'm going to sleep in the study. I was having a nightmare. I don't want to go back to the panelled room.'

'You do that. You sort yourself out. Whatever suits you best.'

With another puzzled, almost frightened glance at the knives in their block, Auntie Sylvia retired upstairs. Elinor took her duvet to the sofa-bed in the study.

She could still hear, far off and terribly faint, the sound of a child crying.

She had won a small, ugly victory, but she was not free. Sooner or later another chance would come, and she would have to take it. She was still horribly afraid but it was a different kind of fear. She was like an animal being led to a slaughter house, quiet and submissive. Soon she would belong entirely to the ghosts that haunted that dark little room with the panelled walls, the windows that never seemed to catch the sun, the old bed with its stifling curtains. She would do whatever they wanted her to do. She would follow the interrupted story again, this time to the bitter end.

Ten

THE FIRST REAL SNOW WAS ON FRIDAY DECEMBER 19th. Oya, burrowed in his haven of blankets, read about Scott's final expedition. He imagined digging himself into an ice cave, to survive the dreadful length of the Antarctic night. The cold of the MacDonalds' spare bedroom bit into his bones. He had to survive until Monday. Then he would be on the plane to Africa. He wouldn't be coming back until January 9th.

He wondered what he could do to keep Lin safe while he was away. Mr Vernon had said, 'Leave it to me', but he obviously hadn't done a thing because Lin was looking as thin and haunted and wild-eyed as ever. Oya had heard that the Christmas season is the worst time for people who are depressed, and though she was a child he knew his friend was as much in need of help as any despairing grown-up. But what could he do?

On Sunday 21st the snow lay deep and crisp and even. The Four Parishes Carol Singers had sung their way round the villages, the houses, the pubs and the outlying farms. Today was the visit to the Hospice. The collecting tins had been well filled this year. The seasonal weather made people feel charitable. There was a party atmosphere at this last gathering, though the real party wouldn't start until after Evensong. The roads were choked with brown slush and many of the lanes still white except where tractors had driven through; but the Singers had turned out in strength. Some came by car, some on foot. Mr Vernon had rounded up the rest in the St Breada's minibus. 'It's going to thaw tomorrow,' he warned them cheerfully, jumping up and down to keep warm as he marshalled his troops in the Hospice car-park. 'Enjoy this while you can!' Oya, who didn't see anything to enjoy, found his way to Elinor's side. She'd arrived with Mrs Madison and her cousins but she stood alone, looking lost. They didn't have a chance to talk: it was time to go in.

'Now let's have the children and less confident singers in the front, big voices in the back where they'll carry; musicians with instruments on the flanks. Are we fit? On we go!'

The Hospice dayroom was still and bright. Garish Christmas decorations seemed like an intrusion, they surely didn't suit any particular resident's taste. But the carol singers massed together and sang, with the clarinets and recorders of the musicians tootling bravely.

God rest you merry gentlemen let nothing you dismay
Remember Christ our Saviour was born this Christmas day . . .

The very ill patients were in their own rooms. The people in the dayroom were not ill, they were simply extremely old, and drifting naturally towards their end. Elinor found herself gazing into the face of an old woman in a burgundy cardigan and pink woollen dress. She looked so incredibly frail and ancient it seemed she might remember the year when little Richard Revelle went missing. Her neck was as thin as a withered flower stalk, her hair a filmy white fleece over her gleaming skull. But she sang along, beating time on the arm of her chair and showing ramparts of oversized false teeth; and her bright eyes looked into Elinor's heart.

God rest ye!

When the singers shuffled off to visit some of the other patients in their rooms, the old lady with the bright eyes beckoned to Elinor.

'Where do you live, my dear?' she asked. Her voice was surprisingly strong.

'I live in the old Dower House, in Breadford,' said Elinor.

'Ah!' She nodded, as if some mystery was explained. 'They could never keep a maid there. Long ago, I remember my grandmother telling how *her* nan went there as a young girl, but she wouldn't stay. My nan's nan didn't like the company she had to keep, though the family that was the tenants then was nice as ninepence.'

'What kind of company?' breathed Elinor. 'What do you mean?'

The ancient lady shook her head, or rather her head shook a little more than it did all the time on that wobbly neck. 'I'm very, very old,' she said. 'When you get as old as I am, you see things different. You see what follows people round, the quiet company folk sometimes have. You see more than the living, maybe. *What kind of company?* I believe you know, my dear . . . God bless you, poor lass. And a Merry Christmas, to all that means no harm –' These final words were spoken as if to someone she could see over Elinor's shoulder. Elinor wanted to ask again, *What can you see?* But one of the hospice nurses had come to collect the stray. She chivvied Elinor away to join the others.

When the final carol was sung they all drove back to Breadford. By the time it was fully dark everyone was gathered at the church. There was no sign of the promised thaw, the sky was thick with more snowfall. The Madisons went back to the Dower House to change for the party, and to collect Uncle Derek, Dekkie, and Auntie Sylvia's avocado-and-passion-fruit vol-au-vents.

Elinor stayed behind. St Breada's was full of flowers and holly branches, shining with electric lights and ranks of candleflames. She knelt and stood and sang along with the people on either side of her. The service passed in a vague dream. She felt that another girl was standing beside her, her coarse frieze jacket brushing Elinor's shoulder, her red rough hands humbly clasped. It was poor Nelly, pleading for release from her torment. And if she could not be released, she would cling forever. She would have company, she would have Elinor to share her agony.

the child crying . . . always crying . . .

Oya, who had not managed to get next to his friend in the crowd, was standing at the back of the church, where the latecomers shuffled from foot to foot and the shadows gathered. He didn't see the silent, inescapable companion at Elinor's side. But he scanned the faces, on the watch for that sinister stalker. The prayers and hymns ended, a rush of bodies started to pour towards the doors: and he saw the person he had been looking for. He saw how the people of Breadford looked uneasy, and left a space around that lady in her full-skirted coat and the hat that shadowed her face, white lace at her throat gleaming in the gloom. They didn't know her, they couldn't work out who she was. He remembered how he had said once, *a ghost might look like an ordinary person.* This lady wasn't ordinary: but could she really be a ghost? He saw the glitter of those hungry eyes and felt sure his friend was in danger. He looked anxiously for Lin, to warn her. When he glanced back, the dark lady had vanished.

Everyone trooped across to the Rectory, laughing and talking. Country neighbours who hadn't seen each other for months exchanged Christmas greetings, cards and little presents. Children were looking forward to the glorious games of hide-and-seek and murder in the dark which Mr Vernon traditionally arranged after supper. Elinor let herself be carried with the rest. She was captured by a tall fourteen-year-old who had spotted her for a newcomer. He began to regale her with stories of the Rectory's spooky reputation.

'It's not as big as the old Revelle place,' he said, 'but it's big. Vicars used to have about twelve children or so, in the old days. There are up and down passages full of shut-up bedrooms: and there are *stories.* I won't tell you some of the things that have happened when we've been playing murder up there in the dark. I don't want to scare you. You'd better stay by me, I'll take care of you.'

Oya worked his way to Elinor's side, and firmly put himself between her and the boy.

'Hi, Rufus, this is my friend Lin. She lives at the Dower House. Lin, this is Rufus Thorne, his sister Freda the horse is a friend of your cousin Nathalie. Don't listen to him. There aren't any ghosts in the Rectory. Not a single one.'

Elinor was staring like a fascinated rabbit. Rufus passed his hand in front of her pale face, she didn't blink. 'Spooooky-dooky babe!' he remarked, and went off in search of easier prey.

'Don't let him bother you,' said Oya. 'He goes to boarding school, poor berk. Never sees a single girl in term time: it makes him pushy.'

Elinor didn't answer. Oya knew his friend was naturally pale, but tonight she looked like death. He felt drowned by responsibility. The vicar and Sonia Manaton were so busy, and he was sure it would be worse than useless to tell Lin's aunt. What could he say? *There's a spooky woman following your niece around.* He decided the best he could do was to stick by Lin until he got a chance to talk to Mr Vernon. At least the stalker, ghost or not, surely wouldn't dare to come into the Rectory.

Little girls and little boys had stripped their woolly outer layers in the Rectory front hall, and emerged like crumpled butterflies in tartan taffeta skirts, fancy waistcoats, satin bow ties. Most of the grown-ups and the older children had not bothered to dress up, but everywhere there were bright sweaters and warm winter colours. Sam Brewer, the giant young organist, was hopefully wearing a sprig of mistletoe behind one ear. Freda Thorne's boyfriend, Ian Davy from Deerhart farm, had made himself a tinsel garland cravat.

Oya spotted Mrs Madison, Nathalie and Megan by the supper table, and winced at the brightness of Nathalie's tiny silver mini-dress. It was well over the top for a Rectory Christmas buffet. That was fine, however. He hadn't spotted Freda Thorne yet, but you could bet she'd be wearing something equally outrageous. And Caroline, too. Mrs Madison's dress, though, was something else! It was long and slinky, in metallic bronze and green, and it had no back. She was wearing about a ton of make-up. No other grown-up in the room was looking anything like so flashy. He wondered, with a rush of relief, if *that* was what was wrong with Lin. Maybe she wasn't spooked. Maybe she was plain mortified by her relations.

He nudged her. 'Hey, before I forget, you look great. I'm glad you didn't dress up, I like that jumper. Don't worry about your aunt, though. Some people always put on party gear, it's okay. Anything goes at this bash. Let's get some food.'

The Rectory's two big drawing rooms had been used for meetings, slide shows and socials since the Village Hall had fallen into disrepair. This evening they were transformed. The folding doors between them had been fastened back, and the waxed floorboards had been polished until they glowed. Holly and ivy boughs were fastened around, a huge mistletoe ball hung from the centre of the front room's ceiling. At one end of the two rooms a Christmas tree stood by the fireplace. At the other, food was spread on long trestle tables covered in white. Oya thought it was like being in a Jane Austen book, at a party where young ladies in slim Regency gowns tripped up and down with partners in breeches and high cravats, while Mr Darcy and his friends made snide remarks, and the country dowagers sat watching everyone with eagle eyes. Except that the company in those days would not have been so mixed, or so noisy. He looked at Elinor, wanting to tell her this. But the words *it's like stepping into the past,* didn't seem well-chosen.

'Come on,' he suggested instead, 'Let's get something to eat.'

His experience as the MacDonalds' paying guest had taught him a great respect for food as medicine. Whatever was wrong, low blood sugar couldn't be helping. He collected two paper plates and elbowed shamelessly to the well-filled tables, Lin following without interest but without resistance. He filled a plate, avoiding some poisonous looking green blobs and concentrating on safe stuff like crunchy free-range chicken legs and Mr Brewer the Baker's splendid sausage rolls. He put it into her hands.

The noise in the big rooms had risen to a happy confused roar. Beside Oya, Mr Vernon and his housekeeper were chatting to two of the doctors from the Group Practice. Dr Simal was an old time Breadford resident. Dr Wright had recently moved from London. The natives were scaring the newcomer with local stories.

'It's the Black Dog you have to watch out for,' Dr Simal assured his colleague. 'Big as a calf, with fiery rolling eyes. One meets it when riding across the moor. More likely, these days, one sees it running by the hedge or crossing the road ahead of one while driving: and then – !' he gestured dramatically, slicing at his own throat with a sausage roll. 'Curtains! You are surely done for.'

'Is that the famous Hound of the Baskervilles?' asked the innocent townie.

'The tale of the Hound of the Baskervilles,' said Dr Simal, winking at Oya, 'is a mere feeble imitation of the true horror that stalks our locality.'

'And then there's the Black Fly Gang,' put in Sonia Manaton. 'Our famous smugglers. They were operating around here from about the middle of the eighteenth century. Several of their number were hung in chains from the old gallows where Black Hill Cross stands now. Our own Wicked Lady's lover was supposed to be among them. They say *she* walks. Yes, it's been reliably reported that she walks in moonlight on Black Hill, gathering his bones.'

'Reliably reported by whom?' asked the new doctor, a nice-looking young woman who was obviously enjoying these ghoulish tales. 'Have you seen her yourself?'

Everybody laughed.

Oya said loudly, 'I think I've seen a ghost! And so's Lin.'

He didn't mean to blurt out these fateful words. His plan had been to take the vicar or Mrs Manaton aside, to tell them again about Elinor's fears and describe the person he'd spotted lurking at the back of the church. But he was close to panic because he was leaving in the morning and he was afraid for Lin, so it came out all wrong. Everybody in the jolly group turned to stare at Lin and Oya: so did the people around them.

'Have you *really*?' demanded the nice lady doctor, excitedly. 'Lucky you! When did it happen? Where did you see it? What did it look like?'

'It's Lin's ghost,' said Oya. 'She'd better tell.'

Lin shook her head. 'No,' she said. 'No. I didn't. I swear I didn't.'

Beyond the trestle table was a big fireplace. Elinor was staring at the wall above it, above the white marble mantelshelf. The grown-ups looked at each other, puzzled by the girl's frightened denial.

'Don't worry,' said Dr Simal kindly, 'We believe you. I expect it was Oya who thought he saw a ghost, and now he's trying to drag you into the story for company!'

Mr Vernon turned, following the direction of Elinor's intense gaze.

'I see you're looking at Deborah Revelle,' he remarked. 'Yes, that's our Wicked Lady, Deborah Revelle in her heyday. If that was a Gainsborough, which is what people often think, we'd be in the money. But I'm afraid that though it's old the portrait is not very valuable. That's why it's still here! Of course, the name and the estate passed away from my branch of the family a long time ago. That picture's one of the few relics I have left.' He grinned at Dr Wright. 'Oya and Lin ought to get in touch with the local tourist office, if they've really seen her. Ghosts are very popular with our summer visitors. In fact, I've thought it might not be a bad idea to pay someone to dress up as Deborah and "walk" on moonlit nights in the season, for a small fee.'

Elinor could not take her eyes from the portrait.

It was Mistress Deborah, in her canary-yellow silk. Her powdered head was held high, her pretty mouth curved in a mocking smile. Her black eyes stared defiance at all the staid and proper Devon folk: and the amber earrings glowed in her ears. Elinor had never been into the Rectory drawing rooms until tonight. She had never seen this picture before, but she knew that gown, its stiff bodice, narrow waist, and the full skirt that flowed and gleamed: an ocean of yellow silk, shimmering with silvery high-lights. She knew Mistress Deborah's little red shoes, she knew the lace that lay on the painted woman's breast, and most of all *she knew that face.* The beautiful young woman in the picture looked down at her with living eyes, her gaze filling Elinor with grief and guilt and horror.

'I didn't do it!' she cried. She thought she was in Eaxby courthouse. The big grave faces of her master and the other solemn gentlemen stared at poor Nelly with awful condemnation. 'I swear to God I didn't do it!'

She fought her way through the crowd and rushed out of the room.

It was dark outside and the snow was falling fast. Elinor ran through the white-shattered night. As soon as she was free from the pictured lady's eyes she was quite calm inside, though she kept up her headlong flight. She knew where she was going. When she reached the road she turned and ran along the churchyard wall until she met the stile where there was a sign pointing the way to St Breada's Tor. That was her way: out on to the moor, where the men of Breadford had searched for Richard Revelle and never found his body. (How she remembered their tramping feet in the Dower House kitchen, the way they had pored over their maps, the howl of the dogs; and Mistress Deborah's haunted black eyes as she watched them come and go . . .) People would search for Elinor, too, but by the time they found her it would be too late. They'd hunt around the Rectory first. Then they'd drive along the lane to the Dower House, peering into hedgerows. Long before they thought of the moor, she would be safe.

She had no coat or jacket. She was drenched through, because the snow was on the edge of thawing and fell in big soft wet flakes. Her feet were numb, she kept slipping on the icy stones. She sat down and pulled off her party shoes and threw them away. That was better. She clambered up the steep path, using her hands, between the dark ghosts of winter trees. She was thinking of peace. It would be so quiet up there in the lonely places. She wouldn't have to worry about the Madisons any more; Oya's anxious eyes would no longer follow her around. She should have understood long ago that this was the real solution. She had been caught in the ghosts' thrall from the beginning. She had never meant to return the amber earrings, never since the first moment she saw them. This was the only way. She had read about death by hypothermia: she hoped it was as easy as it sounded. She would climb on to the moor and walk until she was tired. Then she would lie down in the snow. She would lie down and sleep, for the first time in months. And she would no longer hear the little child who was crying in the dark.

The path met a wall. There was a stile made of jutting stones. Elinor dropped into the snow beside it. She had to rest. But she wasn't safe yet. She had to make herself go on a little further. She clambered up on to the top of the wall. Her hands could scarcely feel the stones. Ahead of her was the open moor. She crouched there on one knee, staring into the whirling whiteness. How vast and shapeless the world was, here above the trees.

Then she saw something moving. She saw a grey shape, through the dancing snow. It was coming towards her. And there was another. They were coming to meet her: a tall woman in a black cloak, a stumbling servant girl and a little boy riding on a grey pony. *They walk*, she remembered. Her dream of peace was destroyed. The ghosts were here. The child, the woman, the friendless maid. They would not leave her alone to sleep. They were waiting for her to join them. Her lips moved. 'No!' wailed Elinor. 'No, stay away from me, let me go!'

She fell backwards off the wall, staggered to her feet and started to run again. She didn't know which way she was heading, she didn't know up from down. She crashed against trees, stumbled on rocks, fought against clinging branches. She did not know how long her flight went on. It ended when she fell against another wall. The snow had stopped. Her head was ringing, her cheeks felt hot, she had no feeling at all in her feet or hands. She stood up, and realised by long familiarity that she was in the home meadow, by St Breada's churchyard. The lights of the big house should be shining through the trees far off, but all was in darkness. She limped through the gateway that appeared in front of her, and saw Mistress Deborah again, waiting for her under the yew tree.

She'd be foolish to think that she could get away. The moor was not for her. Poor Nelly wasn't born for that wide freedom. She must still serve her mistress. Mistress Deborah was waiting beside the Revelle tomb, beside that dip in the ground which had been a pool in summer and was now a slough of mud and ice. Her wide skirts flickered as they brushed the snow. She had come to visit poor Nelly in the Bridewell looking just like that: her head high and her shoulders set. She had brought Nelly a posset in a covered basket, made by her own hands. What a kind mistress, to bring comfort to such a wicked girl . . .

Elinor limped towards her fate. She could hear voices, a dog barking, footsteps in the lane. She thought of the night when she had met her mistress, coming out of the panelled room in riding dress. That was the same night on which poor Diccon did not come home, and Nelly had been distracted by the hue and cry. She had not recalled the strangeness of what she had seen until afterwards. Much later, when that farmer said '*it was not a child that I saw, riding the child's pony*,' she had put things together in her mind. But by then she had known the truth for many days. She had heard a child crying . . .

But she didn't tell.

'I didn't do it,' she whispered, tears springing to her

eyes. At last Elinor knew exactly what Nelly had suffered, and why the poor girl was so tormented.

'I didn't do it. But I didn't tell. I heard my darling crying, but *I didn't tell.*'

The pacing figure turned, and opened wide its arms. At the last moment Elinor screamed. She tried to run. But the ground gave way beneath her and she was falling.

She fell, and lay half stunned in darkness. She was buried alive.

Someone's arms closed around her, and lifted her gently.

'Take him out,' she pleaded. 'Don't leave him here –'

'Who?'

'There's a little boy, he's trapped in here as well. We have to rescue him!'

'Sh, there's no one else. Lie quiet, let me get you out of this.'

'She gave me the yellow ear-bobs,' she whimpered, tears stinging her icy cheeks. 'He cried and cried, but I couldn't tell, because she gave me the ear-bobs. And because I loved her, you see. She didn't love anyone, but I loved my Aunt Deborah –'

'I'm not Deborah,' said a voice that she didn't know – and yet she *did* know it, from somewhere very far and faint in the past. 'I'm Liz. Liz O'Falloren. I'm your mother.'

A short while later, Elinor, having been soaked in a hot bath, dressed in a pair of Sonia Manaton's pyjamas and coaxed into sipping a mug of over-sweetened cocoa, was lying in bed in one of the Rectory's spare rooms. Her mother was sitting beside her, holding her hand. Somewhere else, search parties were being recalled and told the good news. The remains of the Carol Singers' buffet was lying waiting to be cleared away in the morning, Oya had gone back to the MacDonalds, to spend his last night in exile relieved and happy; and the Madisons had returned discomfited to the Dower House.

'Your father's family hated me,' said Liz O'Falloren. She had the deep dimples that Elinor remembered from the lost photograph; and the permanent tan. Her hair was fair, wavy and long, with a few streaks of grey. She looked older. Hatless, without her big coat, she looked nothing like an eighteenth-century ghost. But there was still something outlandish about her, a far away look, as if she belonged under a wider sky. 'I'm a wild colonial girl, and they didn't like my manners. They hated my clothes, my friends and my opinions. When John married me he knew they would never forgive him. Especially not his brother's wife. Your Auntie Sylvia really seemed to hate me for existing, and I must admit I returned the compliment. It didn't matter. We went back to Africa, we were making our lives there: until I got into trouble with the law, when you were just a toddler. I suppose, if the Madisons ever thought about it, that confirmed all their worst suspicions.'

'Why didn't you come?' whispered Elinor. 'When, the fire . . . When Daddy was killed –'

Liz's eyes grew bleak. 'John had taken you back to England,' she remembered. 'Because things were getting scary, the country was moving towards revolution. I couldn't leave. I had a job to do. It was a hard decision, but I had no idea just how much it was going to cost. I ended up in prison. That's where I was when John was killed, and you were supposed to have been killed as well. Things were changing fast in our country by that time, there was a new government and I had friends who were trying hard to help me . . . It still took months for me to get out, and get to England: and all that time I didn't hear a word from John's family. Your Madison grandmother and grandad had moved. We hadn't been in touch with them or with

John's brother. I came to England. I was told that it was all over. Your aunt and uncle had identified the bodies, you were both buried and that was the end of it. I didn't want to see your graves. I left again, straight away. I have no family in England. I didn't want to see the Madisons, and I was sure they didn't want to see me. I know I should have done more. But you were both dead, that was what I had been told from the start. I had no hope, no reason to believe anything else.

'And then, just a couple of months ago, I heard from Oya's parents that they'd had a letter from him about a girl his age whose mother's name was O'Falloren. She was called Elinor, her father had been killed in a fire and she was living with his relatives, a family called Madison. You can imagine, I couldn't believe it was true. But the names were right, and your age was right. I called the hospital where they'd told me you were dead, and that's when I discovered that maybe you really were still alive. I took some leave from my job – I'm a journalist – and came to England at once. I went to the hospital first. I found they had no record of the time I'd come to see them before. I'm not really surprised at that. I'd just walked in off the street, heard what they had to say and walked away again, shell-shocked. But apparently when they'd talked to me the first time they'd been referring to records from the time of the fire – when they thought it was the other little girl, Emily, who had survived. As you know, Emily's parents had been killed too and you'd been rushed across the country to a special burns unit. Eventually the confusion in their records did get sorted out, but by then it was far too late for me. I don't blame the hospital so much. Your aunt and uncle were the ones who knew about me, and I don't understand why they behaved the way they did, when they found out you were still alive . . . ' Liz set her jaw grimly, clearly holding back some bitter, bitter words. 'They say they believed John and I had broken up, and I wasn't interested in you. They say they tried to reach me. It's true I travelled a lot, in the first years after I lost you and John. But I don't think they can have tried very hard.' She shook her head, and changed her tone. 'I went to see Emily's grandmother. I wanted to talk to someone who knew the whole story –'

'She was the one who came,' whispered Elinor. 'I know. They sent for her from Southampton, when they thought I was Emily. We'd changed our clothes, we liked doing that. I was wearing her nightie, she was wearing my pyjamas. When the firemen rescued me, other people living in the flats who knew us said I was Emily. I know that, the nurses at the hospital told me. So they sent for Emily's gran, and she sat holding my hand while I was in intensive care with my face and everything bandaged, and then I woke up and said "*Where's Emily*"?'

'She says she knew,' said Liz. 'She knew all the time it wasn't her granddaughter. But she didn't say anything because she couldn't bear to believe the truth, until you spoke –'

'Oh Mum, they told me Mickey had been killed. My kitten Mickey, he was dead!'

Elinor burst into tears. She remembered! Things that she'd buried deep in her mind came flooding back. And it was as if she had been waiting, all these years, for a chance to cry properly, for Mickey, for Emily; for her dear Daddy. As if her life had been standing still, frozen, unable to get past that terrible accident, until this moment. Her mother rocked her in her arms, crying herself. Then finally she drew back, wiped Elinor's eyes and stroked back the wet strands of hair from her cheeks.

'So there I was,' she said, in a husky voice. 'Eight years too late, a stranger. I didn't think you'd remember me, or miss me.'

'I did!'

'I didn't know that. Derek and Sylvia had been your Mum and Dad all that time, and I knew they detested me. I thought I had no right to appear from nowhere, disrupt your life and try to take you away from everything you knew. I decided I'd see how the land lay before I announced myself. I was scared, to be honest. I took a room in a pub, in Darebridge. I confided in David Vernon, your friend the vicar. He didn't tell me much, but enough. And I watched, and I sized things up.'

Liz O'Falloren's eyes flashed. Elinor heard again the steely tone that had terrified her, when she eavesdropped on Mr Vernon and his mysterious visitor. 'When I saw how sad you looked. When I heard about you being the odd one out, the poor relation, I wanted to beat Derek up. I wanted to punch that woman on the nose. Your Mr Vernon calmed me down. He told me I was scaring you to death, the way I was hanging around. I promised him I'd own up. I came along to the Rectory tonight, to the party. I thought I could trust myself not to thump anyone if it all happened in public. But it didn't work out that way.'

Her grip on Elinor's hand tightened. 'I'm sorry I scared you. Was it really me that made you run like that? I was terrified! Everyone was. Do you know you were out there in the snow for two hours? When they found your shoes on the path to the moor, oh, my heart stopped. I had found you, and lost you again before I could even touch you . . . I stayed in the churchyard, because I was no use to the searchers. Suddenly there you were: and then you disappeared! The ground had caved in by the Revelle tomb, I ran over and found you lying at the bottom of a kind of pit. I'll show you, in the morning. You said something about a little boy, you thought a little boy had fallen in the hole with you. Do you remember? What was that about?'

Elinor didn't want to talk about the ghosts, not now. She shook her head.

'But how did you know Oya's parents?'

Liz laughed. 'I've known Christie and Mashood for ages. We go back a long time. Small world, isn't it? But there's a lot that you don't know about me, Lin, a lot that the Madisons chose not to tell you. I know Christie and Mashood because we've worked together for years, to fight for a good government in our country. My family were settlers in the Asaba hill-country three generations ago, it's the most beautiful country in the world. We stayed on at Independence and I never want to leave. I won't tell you it's easy to be a white African, but I believe in my country. I believe in Africa. I'm an Asaban. And so are you, if you want to be. You were born there. Didn't you know that?' Liz O'Falloren caught herself up: tears were standing in her eyes. 'But hey, make no mistake: if you don't want to leave, I'll stay in England,' she promised. 'I'll fit in with you, you don't have to fit in with me. I'll find a job, we'll get somewhere to live. I don't care what I do, so long as I don't lose you again.'

'Oya could live with us,' murmured Elinor, drifting into sleep, wanting everyone to be included in the miracle of her happiness. 'He hates it at the MacDonalds. They make him feed the alsatians.'

Liz O'Falloren looked taken aback, blinked, and then grinned. 'Well, why not. I'll be a landlady for a while. We'll keep a boarding house for exiled Africans, feed them right and keep them warm. Only you go to sleep now, baby.'

'Don't go away.'

'I won't. Never again.'

Elinor closed her eyes, still holding her mother's hand, still hearing her mother's voice, that strange accent from a far-away land. And the great ocean of sun and air that she had glimpsed, when she drove across the moors with the Madisons one August day, seemed to spread out before her, no longer haunted but full of freedom and promise: a whole new world.

Eleven

'DO YOU BELIEVE ME?'

Elinor had eaten breakfast in bed while her mother sat beside her, showing her photographs and talking about her home in Africa. Then Liz had gone to the Dower House to talk with Derek and Sylvia. She had promised not to thump anyone, but she didn't want Elinor to be around for that conversation. So now Elinor was in Mr Vernon's study, dressed in her clothes from last night, that had been washed and delivered to her warm and dry from the Rectory kitchen range. She had been telling him the whole story of her experiences in the Dower House. This morning, her soul felt spring-cleaned. The idea that she had really come close to killing her cousin Dekkie seemed as ridiculous as the idea that she had actually tried to kill herself. But she had wanted to tell someone, before she left it all behind.

Mr Vernon had been listening carefully, with a few prompting questions. He took off his glasses, and used one of the sidepieces to scratch the back of his neck.

'I think,' he said slowly, 'I think you probably did know the story of Nelly Gipping before you started having those dreams. You were here for two weeks in the summer, and you are a child who reads: I know you are. You had to sleep in that rather sinister old room, and you had found the amber earrings – which I'll be very interested to see, by the way. I think you read the story, and then forgot that you had read it. In some ways your situation was similar to poor Nelly's. I can see that you would want to suppress the conscious memory of what you'd read. You "forgot", but the story came back to you, in dreams in which you seemed to visit the past. The mind does things like that. Do you understand?'

'You think I was going mad?'

'No, I think you were under a lot of stress, more than any of us realised. When that happens the line between make-believe and reality can easily become confused. But I'm wary of believing that you "really" visited the past – though it is a fascinating idea. You see, the records of the events we're talking about are very detailed. I'm afraid that if we examined your account closely, we'd find that you didn't "see" anything on your trips to the past that you couldn't have learned about from reading a local history book or a tourist leaflet.'

'Richard Revelle's body was never found,' said Elinor. 'What if I could find it?'

When she'd been in the middle of the haunting, she'd been afraid that people would try to tell her that she was making up a fantasy based on her own situation. This morning, she would have been very happy to accept a counselling-style explanation, so that she could forget the ghosts. Mr Vernon was unsettling her. She had the impression he was almost ready to believe her whole story, but he was waiting for her to say something that would finally convince him. He put on his glasses. 'Come out to the churchyard,' he suggested.

The snow had vanished overnight, as December snow often does in the West Country. The sun was shining brightly. St Breada's churchyard was a trampled mess from last night's search for Elinor. She followed Mr Vernon to the corner where the yew tree cast its dark shade. He stood looking at the names on the top slab of the Revelle tomb.

Richard Revelle
born 27th March 1780, lost 20th March 1788
His body was never found
The Lord giveth, the Lord taketh away.

Then came a memorial for Simon Revelle his father, and for Francis Revelle, Deborah's son, the one who had ruined the estate. He'd died in his forties. And then, briefly:

Also Deborah, wife of the above Simon Revelle
Born London 1765
Died Breadford 1860

'It's very plain, isn't it,' remarked Mr Vernon, 'for our famous Wicked Lady. But she was the last Revelle to be buried here. Her son was childless, the name around here died with him. So, she has that distinction at least.'

Elinor felt a shock. It seemed to her that she had seen that lovely face, wild and bold and living, only yesterday. 'I didn't realise she died so old.'

'Mmm, very old. A mad, unhappy old woman hated by her respectable daughters, who spent not a penny more than they must on her keep. So they say.'

He pointed to the ground beyond the tomb. It had fallen in, so that there was a hollow pit where the pool had been. A couple of spades and a mattock lay beside it in the mud. Yew roots jutted through its walls, the floor had been turned over and stirred. The muddy earth was scattered with old red needles.

'That's where you fell,' he said. 'Look at the walls. There are signs of stonework. It looks as if there was once a passage leading from the Revelle vault . . . to who knows where? The tunnel is completely blocked, it looks as if it must have fallen in a very long time ago. I suspect this was a smugglers' underground passage. There are other places in Devon where they used the eerie reputation of a churchyard as their protection, and kept kegs of brandy in among the coffins. Last night, your mother tells me you wanted her to rescue a little boy who was in the pit with you? Is that right?'

She nodded dumbly.

'Sam Brewer and Mr Whiddon, my verger, have been up here this morning digging. They found nothing. Do you think we should go on? Did you "see" the lost child buried in this old tunnel? Do you think that's why you saw Deborah Revelle walk?'

Elinor sat on the chilly edge of the Revelle tomb. She felt no horror: it was just St Breada's churchyard. 'I never saw her walk in here until last night, and I'm not sure about that. It was my mother I saw when I thought I was seeing a ghost in the churchyard before. It could have been only my mother last night, though I think it was *both*. Her and the ghost. But most of the time what happened to me wasn't like seeing ghosts, not the way you mean.' She wanted to make things absolutely clear. 'Nelly wasn't dead. It was her life I shared: as if because I was in the same place and I had some troubles that were like hers, I could sort of line up with her. I could feel what she had felt and see what she had seen.' She thought hard. 'There were two, maybe three times that were different, when I saw, or dreamed I saw, an actual ghost in the panelled room. But that was the old lady.'

'Oh yes?' said Mr Vernon in a careful tone, as if he was trying not to sound too interested. 'Could you describe those experiences in details?'

'Didn't I do that already?' She was surprised. 'Maybe I didn't say much because it didn't seem part of the rest. The first night I slept in the fourposter bed, I saw an old lady in a brocade gown. She searched the desk, Diccon's mother's desk, then she got up and walked across the room, and disappeared. I think she was looking for the earrings, but I only guessed that afterwards. When it happened I thought I was having a nightmare. Then once I saw her at the window, and the last time I saw her, she was lying on the bed while I was sleeping on a chair. All three times she ended up doing the same thing. She walked across the room to the same corner, and disappeared. That's all.'

Elinor shuddered. She knew why she hadn't talked much about the old lady. Nothing else had been so hideous, so intolerable as those apparitions.

'What did you say?' Mr Vernon's expression had changed.

'It all happened in the panelled room, not here. That's where we have to –'

'No, no. About the desk. You said something about the desk.'

'The walnut desk. It had belonged to Diccon's mother. I think Diccon must have shown Nelly the hiding place. I think that's why she hid the earrings there: because she knew Aunt Deborah didn't know the secret.'

'That's *very* interesting,' said Mr Vernon, in a tone of wonderment. He pulled off his glasses and twisted the fusewire mend vigorously. 'I believe it's time we went to the Dower House. The family shake-down should be over.'

She knew that she had told him what he had been waiting to hear. But he said no more. They walked to the Dower House. Elinor had borrowed a pair of Mrs Manaton's wellingtons. Mr Vernon was silent on the way, Elinor didn't feel like talking either. The lane was running with melt water. They had to walk down the middle where the grass grew, as if they were treading on stepping stones, to keep out of the worst mud. She noticed, under the ragged leaves of the winter hedgerow, that there were green shoots and crumpled rosettes of primrose leaves. Winter was hardly begun, but the promise of Spring was waiting.

A rather strained atmosphere greeted them, but there was no sign of actual violence. Elinor and her mother and the vicar went to the panelled room. She took the earrings out of their hiding place, and handed them over. He stood, turning them over in his palm, and looking around him. The room felt cold, and sad, and strangely empty of its old oppression. 'Fascinating,' said Mr Vernon. 'I believe you're right, these belonged to the Wicked Lady, these are the earrings in the portrait. You think Nelly Gipping hid them in the desk?'

'She didn't want to die,' said Elinor. 'She took them, because she felt that her aunt had promised them to her if she would keep quiet. I think . . . I hope that she didn't know she was keeping quiet about Diccon's murder, not at first. Aunt Deborah had other secrets. But Nelly's mind wasn't very clear on that. Then when she was accused of murdering Diccon, she didn't want to say anything that would harm Aunt Deborah. But she didn't want to hang, and if the earrings had been found in her possession that would have been proof of a motive. So she managed to hide them. It must have been after they all moved back to the big house, because I don't think that desk was ever in the Dower House in Nelly's day.'

'Nor was the fourposter bed,' agreed Mr Vernon. 'It would have been brought here, with the desk, about fifty years later, when Nelly was long dead and Deborah Revelle an old woman. That was when the Dower House was brought into service again, after standing empty for a long time.' He smiled at Elinor, looking apologetic. 'Once, back in the summer, you told me you were sleeping in the fourposter room, and I'm afraid I kept quiet about something I thought you didn't need to know! Deborah Revelle died in this room, in that bed. She spent the last years of her life here: old and confused and almost a prisoner. What's more, there *was* once a family tradition that this room was haunted by the old lady, just as you described her. I suppose that may even be why, when the Dower House was partially renovated as a holiday home, Deborah's room was left untouched and shut up, along with this whole wing.' He pulled off his glasses again, and twisted the wire-mend. 'Well, this is extraordinary. Possibly you could have learned everything you know about Nelly Gipping's story from local history publications. *I* didn't tell you about the old lady's ghost, but you might have heard about that from somewhere, and seen what you expected to see. And I suppose it is *just possible* you could have got hold of an eighteenth-century inventory of the first Mrs Simon Revelle's possessions, because such a thing exists, I have seen it myself, in the county museum archives. So you could have known the desk was Diccon's mother's, without having travelled in time –'

'As long as I don't have to sleep here again,' said Elinor wryly. 'I don't mind what you believe.'

She was thinking, so the old lady with the terrible eyes had been Aunt Deborah. She was what Aunt Deborah had become. And in spite of everything, she felt sorry for the Wicked Lady. But she was not afraid, not anymore. She had not heard the child crying since last night. She was lightheaded with the knowledge, the sure promise that she would never hear that terrible weeping again. But there was still something to be done. She wondered how she was going to persuade them . . .

'No! cried Mr Vernon losing patience with himself. 'No! I can't believe it! It's too much. I think I have to believe *you*, instead, Elinor. I'm going to have to believe in ghosts. Somehow these things are possible: rare but possible. You said to me, back at the Rectory, that you thought you could find Richard Revelle's body. What did you mean by that?'

'I don't know where he is,' she said. 'But he must be very near this room. Because Nelly,' her voice broke, 'she could hear him crying. I could hear him crying, all the time . . .'

'I think we should stop this,' broke in Liz O'Falloren, going to her daughter.

'No,' Elinor shook her head. She knew she had to keep on, until the end. 'I'm all right.'

Mr Vernon was walking round the room the way Elinor had done on her first night, feeling up and down the panelling. 'I *wonder*,' he muttered. 'I wonder . . . How extraordinary, if we could clear up a two hundred-odd-year-old murder mystery!' He reached the corner by the door. 'This is where she disappeared?'

'Yes.'

The wall did not sound hollow when knocked. But Mr Vernon was determined now.

'I think we might have a look behind,' he remarked. 'Let's consult the owners.'

Uncle Derek and Auntie Sylvia were called in. They put up no resistance to the suggestion that the panels in that corner should be taken down. They were rather thrilled. Mr Vernon called up Sam Brewer and the verger. They soon arrived, in a van with a carpenter and tools. Mrs Manaton came with them. It would have been impossible to get hold of any workmen for ordinary purposes, at short notice on the Monday before Christmas. But the mention of ghosts and secret passages had worked like magic.

Nathalie, Megan and Derek piled in, it was no longer possible to keep them out. Everyone watched in tense silence as Mr Gurney the carpenter examined the panelling again, with an expert eye. He discovered that they would not have to use violence. One of the oaken roses, in a band of floral carving at head height, had a boss in the centre that moved slightly under pressure. After some persuasion, the whole panel slid away. There was a door beyond. It was very thick, which explained why they had not been able to hear a hollow sound. 'I've seen this kind of thing before,' said the carpenter. 'Around Dartmoor. Priest's holes, smugglers' passages. Only one or two folk would be in the secret when the hidden room or passage was installed. If something happened to prevent those key people from passing the information on, the secret could soon be lost completely. I've never heard of a passage in the Dower House, but I'm not surprised. It's a very old place, seen some rum times.'

The men crowbarred the rust-fused lock, and the massive door opened inwards. There were steps leading down. Mr Gurney asked them all to stay back, and ventured into the cold musty dark with his big flashlight. After a moment they heard him say, quietly, 'Vicar, come and have a look at this here. Looks like human remains. Looks like it was a child.'

Richard Revelle was found.

Mrs Manaton firmly ordered the Madisons to take their children away, and went with them to make sure they didn't sneak back to peep and pry at the creepy bones. Human remains must not be touched, not disturbed at all, until they had been properly examined. Elinor was afraid that she'd be sent away, too. But Mr Vernon understood. When he and Mr Gurney came back, the men waited above while Elinor and her mother went down the steps.

He was lying in a corner of the small, windowless bare room, huddled up at the foot of another door. The ancient timbers bulged inward under the pressure from the fallen tunnel roof beyond. Elinor felt as if her mouth was full of earth. How did Nelly manage to hear the child crying, through the thick, muffling barrier of the secret door? Maybe she didn't hear, she just knew. This room and the passage beyond must have been forgotten by the Revelle family, because Simon had not known about it. But Deborah Revelle had found out the secret, and realised how it could be used. She had locked her husband's son in here and pretended he was lost on the moor, so that her own children would inherit; and maybe to protect her double life. Only poor Nelly, who had died before she could be put on trial, had guessed or known the truth about Diccon's death. Elinor wondered, did Simon Revelle ever suspect his wife? Perhaps he did, but could never bear to accuse her. But Deborah had paid the price for her crimes in the end. She had been put away herself, in the very room that held the secret of Diccon's death. She could not tell anyone about the horror she must have felt. She had suffered in a living grave for years, haunted by dreams of the poor girl she had betrayed, and tormented by the sound of a child, crying . . .

The pity of the little boy's fate overwhelmed her. Alone and in the dark, sobbing and pleading for someone to come, until he was too weak to cry any more. Tears were running down her face. She didn't try to stop them.

'Poor child,' said Liz, in her forthright way. 'What a rotten way to go.' She put her arm around her daughter's shoulders, and led her back into the light and air.

Some time later, they went out and drove for miles in Liz's hired car. Liz didn't say a word until they were up on top of the moor. She stopped in the car park opposite a roadside pub. It was a beautiful day. There was snow lingering on the High Tors. The moorland stretched wide, whale-backed and severe to every horizon: forever and ever and ever.

Elinor took the pouch holding the amber earrings out of her pocket, and emptied them on to her palm. Mr Vernon had said that he thought she could keep them. They had been sold with the Dower House. He thought they had no 'rightful owner' but herself. She didn't know yet what she would do. She didn't know if she could bear to keep such a reminder of the nightmare. Maybe she should give them to the museum in Eaxby.

'Nelly saw her,' she said quietly. 'The day Diccon was supposed to have gone out riding, Deborah dressed in a man's riding clothes and rode his pony up on the moor and left it there. Nelly saw her dressed like that, coming out of the panelled room: and later, when a farmer said the pony's rider 'didn't look like a child', she put two and two together. I wonder if Deborah was really in league with the smugglers, and they were part of the plot to kill Diccon? It would explain the flies in the earrings. They were called the 'Black Fly Gang', or something like that.'

'It seems likely enough,' agreed Liz, tucking her gloved hands in her pockets and huddling down into the caped collar of her big coat. Like Oya, she couldn't bear the cold. Elinor was grateful for her patience. This morning she'd felt half sure she was confessing a horrible fantasy to Mr Vernon. Now the ghosts were real. It helped to talk about them.

'I think she killed Nelly, too. She visited Nelly in prison, and took her "something to make her sleep", but it was something to make her sleep and never wake up. It was easy for her to visit, pretending she was being Christian and forgiving. And I know she had those strong sleeping powders the doctor had given her, after Diccon disappeared . . . Mum?'

She wasn't used to using the word, it made her voice tremble.

'Yes?'

'They were living people. I never completely believed that. Even at the worst, deep down I thought it was all in my head. But when I saw those little bones . . . ! There's something I've remembered, that I haven't told anybody. The first night, after I'd seen the old lady, I heard a child come into the room. I was *terrified.* I think Deborah Revelle, when she was old and dying in that bed, must often have imagined Diccon was there with her, and I was feeling the way she had felt. But then I thought it was Dekkie, so of course I stopped being afraid. He was just a child, coming to me for comfort . . . So I hugged him, and comforted him. I wish I could think that it helped. Helped Deborah, I mean. If you had seen her eyes, Mum. She was an awful person, but to think of someone feeling like that for two hundred years! I wish I could think I helped.'

'That sounds like a question for David Vernon,' said Liz, carefully. 'But if you're going to believe in ghosts, I don't see why you can't believe they exist for some good reason. Although it cost you a lot of grief, it seems as if maybe you were needed here.'

'What happened to me was real,' whispered Elinor, wiping her eyes.

'Yes,' said her mother. She didn't say *but it's over now.* She didn't say *put it out of your mind*, or any of those sensible, grown-up things. Because bad things happen and they must not be denied, or they will never be made good.

The carpark was surprisingly full. Christmas season tourists were strolling on the edge of the moorland, and there was even an ice-cream van. Liz pointed to it. She opened the car door. Bright, cold air burst in on them.

'Come on,' she said. 'I'll buy you a big fat snowcone.'

I'll never forget you, promised Elinor silently as she

followed her mother to the cheery pink and white van. Now she knew she would keep the yellow ear-bobs, in memory of little Diccon, and poor Nelly, and lovely, terrible Aunt Deborah. Those three shadows would be with her forever. They seemed more real than Aunt Sylvia or any of the Madisons, who were already fading into the dim album-pages of unimportant memory. But the sun was shining, and her mother had found her again. She had done what the ghosts wanted her to do, and she was free.

For readers who like to get back to the sources:

The ghost story in this novel, especially the apparition of the old lady, was inspired by a very scary story by Sheridan LeFanu, called *Madam Crowl's Ghost*, which you will find in the collection of the same name, first published in 1923 and recently reprinted by Wordsworth Classics. Good ghost hunting. *A. H.*

Other books by Ann Halam

The Powerhouse

'The face looked at Maddy. I saw its empty eyes gleam . . . Somebody screamed and screamed. I think it was me.'

Robs, Jef and Maddy: three friends who just wanted to make music together. How could one summer change their lives the way it did? Maddy and Robs survived, but only just, and the nightmare that happened in the Powerhouse will live with them for ever.

'superbly packaged horror' *Books Magazine*

'worth twenty Point Horrors' *School Librarian*

The Fear Man

A dreadful secret hangs over the house in Roman Road. What is it that keeps drawing Andrei to it? And what is the unknown presence that seems to be stalking the family? Constantly on the run from a father he has never known, Andrei is living a nightmare. A compelling story of vampires, magicians and creatures of darkness.

'brilliantly written . . . . a very powerful and affecting book' *BBC Radio 4 Treasure Islands*

The Haunting of Jessica Raven

'Darkness. A cold, foul-smelling darkness. Somewhere a child was screaming.'

Mysterious things start happening to Jessica when, on holiday in France, she meets a strange group of ragged children. She cannot work out where they come from, but when she meets their leader, an older boy called Jean-Luc, she begins to realize that they may hold the key to her brother's fatal illness.

'a novel of singular completeness and perfection. With it Ann Halam confirms her standing as one of the most exciting of emerging talents.' *Junior Bookshelf*